W9-BDQ-389

She was definitely all grown up

But she was still Beth, and he had to remember that. She wasn't like the women he usually dated. Beth was a forever kind of girl. He frowned at the thought of the ex-husband he'd never met. But Zach didn't have to meet him to know he didn't like him. Anyone who hurt Beth was his enemy.

Zach clenched his jaw. No matter how much he was attracted to her, he would never, ever take advantage of her. Beth meant too much to him. Even if a misguided need for revenge or an urge to prove she could seduce him started her thinking along those lines, he would not allow it to happen. He almost laughed at that. Wishful thinking on his part. There was no denying what he still felt. But…he would protect her just as he always had.

He would protect her from him.

For the most private investigations.

Dear Reader,

It's hot outside. So why not slip into something more comfortable, like a delicious Harlequin American Romance novel? This month's selections are guaranteed to take your mind off the weather and put it to something much more interesting.

We start things off with Debbi Rawlins's *By the Sheikh's Command*, the final installment of the very popular BRIDES OF THE DESERT ROSE series. Our bachelor prince finally meets his match in a virginal beauty who turns the tables on him in a most delightful way. Rising star Kara Lennox begins a new family-connected miniseries, HOW TO MARRY A HARDISON, and these sexy Texas bachelors will make your toes tingle. You'll meet the first Hardison brother in *Vixen in Disguise*—a story with a surprising twist.

The talented Debra Webb makes a return engagement to Harlequin American Romance this month with *The Marriage Prescription*, a very emotional story involving characters you've met in her incredibly popular COLBY AGENCY series from Harlequin Intrigue. Also back this month is Leah Vale with *The Rich Girl Goes Wild*, a not-to-be-missed billionaire-in-disguise story.

Here's hoping you enjoy all we have to offer this month at Harlequin American Romance. And be sure to stop by next month when Cathy Gillen Thacker launches her brand-new family saga, THE DEVERAUX LEGACY.

Best,

Melissa Jeglinski
Associate Senior Editor
Harlequin American Romance

THE MARRIAGE PRESCRIPTION
Debra Webb

TORONTO • NEW YORK • LONDON
AMSTERDAM • PARIS • SYDNEY • HAMBURG
STOCKHOLM • ATHENS • TOKYO • MILAN • MADRID
PRAGUE • WARSAW • BUDAPEST • AUCKLAND

If you purchased this book without a cover you should be aware
that this book is stolen property. It was reported as "unsold and
destroyed" to the publisher, and neither the author nor the
publisher has received any payment for this "stripped book."

I would like to thank a very special friend of mine by
dedicating this book to her. She helps me keep my feet
planted firmly on the ground. She makes me laugh and I
enjoy her company, and her writing advice, immensely.
Knowing this fabulous lady has truly added a new value
and depth to my life. Martha Krieger, this one is for you.

ISBN 0-373-16935-3

THE MARRIAGE PRESCRIPTION

Copyright © 2002 by Debra Webb.

All rights reserved. Except for use in any review, the reproduction or
utilization of this work in whole or in part in any form by any electronic,
mechanical or other means, now known or hereafter invented, including
xerography, photocopying and recording, or in any information storage
or retrieval system, is forbidden without the written permission of the
publisher, Harlequin Enterprises Limited, 225 Duncan Mill Road,
Don Mills, Ontario, Canada M3B 3K9.

All characters in this book have no existence outside the imagination of
the author and have no relation whatsoever to anyone bearing the same
name or names. They are not even distantly inspired by any individual
known or unknown to the author, and all incidents are pure invention.

This edition published by arrangement with Harlequin Books S.A.

® and TM are trademarks of the publisher. Trademarks indicated with
® are registered in the United States Patent and Trademark Office, the
Canadian Trade Marks Office and in other countries.

Visit us at www.eHarlequin.com

Printed in U.S.A.

ABOUT THE AUTHOR

Debra Webb was born in Scottsboro, Alabama, to parents who taught her that anything is possible if you want it badly enough. She began writing at age nine. Eventually she met and married the man of her dreams and tried some other occupations, including selling vacuum cleaners and working in a factory, a day-care center, a hospital and a department store. When her husband joined the military, they moved to Berlin, Germany, and Debra became a secretary in the commanding general's office. By 1985 they were back in the States, and they finally moved to Tennessee, to a small town where everyone knows everyone else. With the support of her husband and two beautiful daughters, Debra took up writing again, looking to mystery and movies for inspiration. In 1998 her dream of writing for Harlequin came true. You can write to Debra with your comments at P.O. Box 64, Huntland, Tennessee 37345.

Books by Debra Webb

Don't miss any of our special offers. Write to us at the following address for information on our newest releases.

Harlequin Reader Service
U.S.: 3010 Walden Ave., P.O. Box 1325, Buffalo, NY 14269
Canadian: P.O. Box 609, Fort Erie, Ont. L2A 5X3

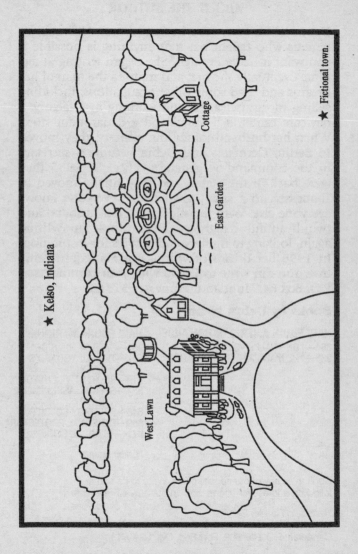

★ Kelso, Indiana

West Lawn

East Garden

Cottage

★ Fictional town.

Prologue

More than three decades ago...

The three women sat in the elegant parlor, two on the original Sheraton sofa, one in a stately wing-back chair on the opposite side of an exquisite Chippendale table. Tea sat cooling in its gleaming silver pot, the one the lady of the house used for very special visitors. And today's visitor was the most special of all.

An expectant silence had filled the air for far too long before someone finally spoke. "I think this is the best solution for everyone," she said with a smile that masked the inner turmoil she didn't want the others to see. Bringing these two together was the perfect solution. She glanced at her dear friend who sat at her side. It could work. She knew it could.

"I agree, my friend," the oldest of the three added in that refined tone polished by years of finishing school. "I can assure you that if you choose this solution," she said to the youngest, "the child will never want for anything. Never. The finest health care and schooling will be provided, regardless of cost. The child will have the best of everything, including parents that will love him or her with all their hearts.''

She noticed the tears in her dear friend's eyes as she spoke and she blinked furiously to hold back her own. This was the right thing to do. It was in the best interest of all concerned. How could any of them lose? They couldn't. She would not have arranged this meeting otherwise.

''I—I know both of you are right,'' the young woman said hesitantly. She was eighteen, unmarried and pregnant…she was desperate. The baby's father was missing in action, presumed dead. ''It's just that this is so hard.'' Her own tears welled past her lashes and rolled down her pale cheeks. She placed her palm against her still flat abdomen and seemed to gather her courage. ''But this is the best way. I know that. My child will be better off with you.'' She smiled faintly through her tears. ''So, how do we do this?''

The oldest of the three smiled warmly, anticipation lighting her eyes. ''Don't worry dear, we'll take care of everything. You won't ever have to worry again.''

Chapter One

He had no choice.

For the first time in his adult life, Zach Ashton was going to have to put his personal life before his professional one. And it wasn't an easy task. His natural inclination was career first, and anything else worth having would follow. It was the law by which all Ashtons lived.

"You're sure two weeks won't be a problem?" Zach paused in his restless pacing to study his longtime boss, Victoria Colby, as she considered his question.

"I'm quite sure. You should take as much time as you need. We'll be fine here."

He braced his hands on the backs of the two wing chairs flanking her massive oak desk and blew out a weary breath. "Johnson and Wilks have everything under control," he said as much to himself as to Victoria. "They have my mother's number if they need me for anything."

Victoria searched his face with that assessing gaze of hers and then hit the nail right on the head. "Who are you trying to convince, Zach, me or you?"

Moving around one of the chairs, he dropped into

it and leaned his head against its high back. "Me, I think." He settled his gaze on Victoria's then. "She's the only family I have left, and I love her. I can't *not* go." He scrubbed a hand over his jaw. He'd agonized over this decision all night. "A week from Saturday is her birthday for Christ's sake. I have to be there. But two weeks?" He shook his head. "Can I tolerate two whole weeks without the rush of a legal coup?"

Victoria flared her palms. "You said yourself that considering your mother's recent heart attack and her age, you couldn't afford not to go for an extended visit."

Zach nodded. "Seventy-five's a major milestone. And the heart attack scared the hell out of me. I have to stay the whole two weeks. I'm just not sure either of us will survive it. We're both too accustomed to having our way."

Victoria smiled with understanding. She, of all people, knew Zach rarely took no for an answer when he wanted something. He'd inherited that tenacious trait from his mother.

"Forget work," Victoria suggested. "Enjoy your mother. Let this be her time. Acquiesce to her every demand. Who knows? Maybe you'll have more fun than you expect."

He arched a skeptical brow. "In Kelso, Indiana? Population not nearly enough. I doubt it." Zach stood. "But I'll go."

"Good." Victoria rose from her chair. "I'll see you in two weeks then."

Zach hesitated at the door and produced a feigned smile. "And I'll enjoy every minute of it if it kills me."

There was a very good chance it would, Zach didn't add as he slipped out of his boss's office and closed the door behind him. He hadn't spent more than a day or two at one time back home in too many years to remember. It was true that part of the reason was the fact that he and his mother were so very much alike, both determined to do things their own way. But Zach dearly loved his mother and he always deferred to her wishes. Always. She had taught him to go after what he wanted with a vengeance, and to never say die. Like any good son, Zach had learned his lesson well. Only once in his entire life had he backed away from what he really wanted. And therein lay the other part of the reason he rarely went home for a lengthy stay.

But he didn't know why he was worried so much about it, *she* wouldn't be there anyway.

"You TELL that old battle-ax that I wouldn't coordinate her birthday party now if she begged me to!"

Beth McCormick stared, appalled, at her mother, then turned her attention to her mother's employer. "Mrs. Ashton, I'm sure Mother didn't mean to say battle-ax. You'll have to forgive her, she's been under a lot of stress lately, and—"

"You're darned tootin' I meant battle-ax," Helen McCormick argued, her dark eyes glittering with anger. She stood now, her fists planted firmly on her hips. "I'm washing my hands of the whole affair!"

Other than the red tingeing her cheeks, Colleen Ashton showed little outward reaction to her oldest friend's outburst. Calmly, Colleen turned her regal head in Beth's direction and smiled patiently. "Beth, if *she* chooses to resign her post as chairperson of my birthday party, it's perfectly all right with me. I'm quite certain that the event will be a great deal more appealing and fresh without an old bag like her running the show anyway.''

Helen's eyes bulged with indignation. "Why I ought to—"

"Mother." Beth jumped to her mother's side and tugged her toward the parlor door. "We'll get this all straightened out, Mrs. Ashton. Don't worry about anything. Your birthday will be everything you've dreamed it would be."

Colleen rose, not a single elegant feather appearing ruffled. "I'm sure you'll do a much better job than your mother."

Beth stalled halfway to the door. She couldn't mean... "But I—"

"Don't worry, dear," Colleen assured her, "Zach is arriving this afternoon. He'll be more than happy to help you make all the arrangements. We won't need anyone else," she added with a pointed stare at her old friend.

Helen McCormick glared at Colleen Ashton, but to her credit she didn't retaliate. Not verbally anyway. Instead, she stamped out of the room, down the entry hall and out the front door, slamming it firmly behind her.

Beth shrugged, uncertain what to say. Opting to remain silent for fear of unintentionally volunteering for something else she'd regret, Beth rushed out of the house to catch up with her mother.

"Mother!" Beth dashed across the porch and down the steps, then matched her stride to her mother's furious one. "What in the world was that all about?"

"I have nothing else to say on the subject," Helen snapped, then compressed her lips into that firm line that indicated the depth of her fury much more so than anything she could have said. Whatever had happened, Beth's usually unflappable mother was fit to be tied.

"This is ridiculous," Beth insisted. "You and Mrs. Ashton have been friends for a lifetime. What could possibly have happened to cause such a falling out?"

Helen stopped abruptly and turned to face her daughter. With her gray hair in its usual neat style, and wearing her jeans and work shirt, both meticulously pressed, she looked just as she always did—serene, earthy. But something was very, very wrong.

Beth's mother had been head housekeeper and cook in the Ashton home for forty years. She'd been overseer of the estate grounds as well since Beth's father died. Although she no longer did much of the actual work herself, no one dared to challenge Helen's authority when it came to the care and keeping of the house or the property. Not to mention she'd been companion to and best friends with the mistress of the estate for most of that same forty years. Never in Beth's entire life had she seen these two old friends at odds like this.

Never.

"Let's just say that there are some things that need to be said, and it's not my place to do the saying," Helen told her without telling her anything at all.

With that, she stormed across the driveway and up the stone path of the east garden to her cottage.

Beth stared after her until she'd disappeared inside. Exasperated, Beth considered the small, inviting cottage in which she had grown up. Ivy partially covered the gray stone walls, while the east garden provided a picturesque setting with its array of rose bushes and other flowering shrubs that Beth's father had seen to the nurturing of for nearly half a century. Ancient trees stood majestically above the wood-shingled roof, the heavy green boughs blending with those of the dense woods scarcely fifty yards behind the cottage. On the south side towered one massive old tree in particular that held fond memories for Beth. The giant oak on whose sturdy branch her father had hung her first swing with its wooden seat and heavy braided rope cables. The very one still hanging there today.

The memory of laughing as Zach Ashton pushed her ever higher in that swing flooded her being. She closed her eyes and relived the feel of the wind on her face, the sound of his deep, rich laughter. Though much older than she, he'd proven a reliable friend and even an occasional playmate. Beth opened her eyes and grimaced at the memory. Zach would likely consider that time with her more baby-sitting duty than playtime. The worst part was that she had been in love with him since she was twelve years old.

She'd watched him graduate from high school and go off to law school, and in her heart of hearts she'd known that when he finished his education he'd come back for her.

But he hadn't.

He'd come back all right, but not for her.

So certain of their future together that at seventeen, she'd felt compelled to show him once and for all just how much she loved him. Beth cringed now at the thought. Zach had come home for a weekend visit and she'd thrown herself at him, professing her love and offering him her innocent, young body.

He had refused.

Beth took a deep breath and shoved those thoughts and the hurt that still accompanied them way back into a dark corner where they belonged. This was not the time to dawdle in the past. She had to find a way to patch the rift between her mother and Zach's. Otherwise she was going to be stuck organizing this birthday party.

Her eyes widened as Mrs. Ashton's final words sank fully into her head. Zach would be here this afternoon.

Today.

Oh, God.

Beth's stomach quivered and her knees felt suddenly weak. Now, she decided, would be an excellent time for her to take a vacation anywhere but here. But she couldn't. She had patients depending upon her. One in particular.

"Okay, girl, you can do this." Beth took another deep breath and forced her feet in the direction of home.

This wouldn't be the first time Zach had come home for a brief visit. It wasn't as if she hadn't seen him in all this time since he'd brutally broken her young heart. She'd seen him several times. Even exchanged hellos and how are yous. She halted midstep.

But she hadn't seen him since…

…the day she'd announced her impending marriage.

…a marriage that had proven a huge mistake.

Wasn't she the picture of success? Thirty-one, divorced and living with her mother. God, she was pathetic.

Beth squared her shoulders. This was the new millennium. Divorce wasn't a disease and living with her mother wasn't a measure of her lack of success in life. Both simply were.

Besides, Zach Ashton was just a childhood memory...a local legend in these parts. The richest, most eligible bachelor in Higdon County. All the girls had loved him. But that was then and this was now. Beth grinned impishly. The guy was a lawyer. She knew plenty of lawyers. He was probably overweight, balding and sporting reading glasses.

She hadn't seen him in...five years? That was about right. He'd come home briefly when Mrs. Ashton had been hospitalized following her heart attack, but Beth had been away participating in a medical conference at the time. And since she'd only been living with her mother for four months, her schedule and Zach's, as far as the couple of visits he'd made, had not coincided.

She felt immensely better now. Beth started toward the cottage again. She might be divorced and living at home with her mother, but she had kept her figure. In fact, she took excellent care of herself. She ran three miles everyday and worked out, was still lucky to have great skin and not the first sign of gray hair. And her salary as a physician allowed her to invest wisely and to dress well.

Well, usually she dressed well.

Today being an exception since she was helping her mother in the garden and wasn't on call. At sixty-five, Helen was slowing considerably, but she refused to allow the gardener to come near the roses—

roses Beth's father had planted. She smiled. Since she was living at home now, the least she could do was give her mother a hand from time to time. Besides, she'd always loved to play in the flowers. And jeans and T-shirts were still her favorite off-duty attire. She could care less if the president himself was stopping by this afternoon. Beth had no intention of behaving any differently than she always did.

The sound of a car pulling into the drive brought her up short. She turned around slowly and shaded her eyes from the sun with her hand. *Please don't let this be him, Lord,* she pleaded. *I know I just said I didn't care, but it was a little white lie. I need to be prepared before I face the man.*

A red sports car braked to a stop and the driver climbed out and stretched as if he'd been sitting too long. Though she didn't recognize the car, Beth had that feeling. He turned toward her. Her heart stilled during the hesitation that followed. Then, as if finally recognizing her, a brilliant smile broke out across his face.

It was him.

"Beth!"

Zach Ashton strode in her direction and her heart felt as if it had stopped beating entirely...which was impossible since she didn't drop dead.

He was not fat.

Or balding.

Or wearing reading glasses.

He was perfect. Just like all those years ago, only better. He was tall, lean and absolutely gorgeous. His khakis might be slightly travel wrinkled, but the navy blue polo shirt that molded to his perfect pecs and broad shoulders more than made up for it.

He stopped directly in front of her, pulled off his designer sunglasses and hugged her fiercely.

He smelled like fresh air and sandalwood. And his strong arms felt like heaven around her. For about two seconds she resisted the urge to press her cheek to his chest and then she gave in. He'd held her just like this a hundred times before. When she'd cried after Sammy Potter pushed her down on the playground. When she'd gotten her period at eleven and realized she had to be a girl whether she wanted to or not. And then, at sixteen when her father had died and she'd been devastated.

Eventually Zach drew away and stared down at her, his hands still bracketing her waist. "God, you look great."

Color shot to her cheeks. She did not look great. She had on jeans and a T-shirt and worn-out sneakers. She was sweaty and dusty from puttering in the garden with her mother.

She was—darn it—she was a mess.

"Hi, Zach," she managed to croak. "You look…terrific."

Boy did he. His hair was shorter, but still dark and thick. Those eyes. She melted just looking into them. As clear and blue as when he'd been twenty-two and visiting from college. And his face. How could anyone so close to forty still look that damn good? There was a line or two here and there, but they only gave him character.

"God, I've missed you," he said wistfully. "What are you doing here? Visiting your mom?"

This was it. Insecurity riddled what was left of her bravado. She was divorced, living with her mother and…God Almighty…still in love with Zach Ashton.

"No," she admitted, the word seeming to ring out in the otherwise silence that surrounded them. "I'm living here again. I'm on staff at Cartersville General."

He looked stunned.

She felt humiliated.

"I thought you were—"

She shook her head, cutting him off before he could utter the M-word. "Not anymore." Apparently their two mothers had kept their word about not mentioning Beth's marital woes.

Zach took her left hand in his and stared at her bare ring finger. He frowned. "I'm…" his concerned gaze reconnected with hers "…sorry."

Beth manufactured a smile. "I'm not." She stepped out of his hold. "Your mother's inside. I'm sure she can't wait to see you."

He nodded distractedly. "Yeah." He hitched a thumb toward his car. "I should get my bags."

Beth blinked. "Bags?"

That devilish grin that had charmed every female in this county as well as the next spread across his devastatingly handsome face. "Didn't she tell you? I'm taking a little time off. I'll be here for two weeks. That's why I drove instead of taking a flight."

Two weeks?

Beth couldn't take two weeks of having him right next door. The past was bound to come up. He'd want to talk. She'd want to…she slammed the door on that notion.

"I thought maybe I could help with the birthday organizing," he added when she didn't respond.

"That'd...be great," she forced out. "Just great."

He started to back away, those amazing blue eyes never leaving hers. "Let's have dinner or something," he suggested in that sexy, utterly male way that came as naturally as breathing to him.

"Sure," she lied.

Dinner was out of the question. She couldn't have dinner with him. She couldn't have anything with him. What was she thinking? Blast it all, it was like she was a teenager again and unable to think properly in his presence.

He was halfway to his car before he finally turned his back to her, but before he did, he shook his head and exhaled a big breath of genuine masculine approval. "You look...terrific. It's *really* good to see you."

Beth managed to keep her smile in place until he'd turned around. Then it collapsed into a ground-dragging frown. Only then, with his mesmerizing attention focused elsewhere, did her heart stumble back into an acceptable rhythm.

She was doomed.

Doomed to replay her tortured teenage years when she'd lived and breathed Zach Ashton.

Whatever it took, she had to get her mother and Mrs. Ashton back on speaking terms. Living next door to Zach for two whole weeks would be bad enough. No way was she going to organize an event the size of this birthday celebration with him. That would mean hours of going over decorations, music, menu selections and sending out invitations—which was only a formality anyway since folks around here planned their Septembers around Mrs. Ashton's birthday.

Beth sprinted the rest of the way to the cottage. All she had to do was find out what had started it. Then she could prod the two old friends into making up. They'd been friends an eternity without the first ripple.

How hard could it be to straighten out this little misunderstanding?

SHE WAS HERE.

And she was even more beautiful than ever. To top it off, she was not only all grown-up, she was available. Zach took a long, deep breath and forced his thoughts away from Beth. He never could think straight around her.

Determined to get past the shock of seeing her, he made his grand entrance into the house only to find that his mother was sleeping. Betty, the housekeeper, said that Mrs. Ashton had retired for a brief nap before the arrival of her son.

Deciding his mother needed the rest and that he could get settled in the meanwhile, Zach lugged his bags up the stairs. He deposited them into his old room and then eased quietly to his mother's door at the other end of the hall. He smiled as he watched her sleep for a moment. Even at seventy-five she was a lovely woman. He inhaled the scent of *White Shoulders* and surveyed the familiar room. It looked just as it had when he'd been a child. Elegant and luxurious. His mother's taste was impeccable. And beneath that pretentious appearance beat a tremendously caring heart. The whole town loved and respected her. She was the best mom a guy could ask for.

Suddenly feeling glad to be home, Zach soundlessly closed the door and made his way back to his own room. He took a deep breath and studied the past that was well documented in the unchanged décor. Football trophies, team photographs and banners covered the walls. Memorabilia of family vacations was scattered about on bookshelves and the tops of his dresser and chest of drawers. Zach picked up a picture of his father and smiled sadly. Graduation day from law school. His father had been so proud. Zach still missed him, though he'd been gone for more than a decade.

Zach carefully placed the picture back on his dresser and wandered to the double windows on the other side of the room. He leaned against the window frame and watched Mrs. McCormick and Beth in the rose garden.

She'd been so gorgeous all those years ago when she'd kissed him. Heat stirred inside him at the memory of her sweet young body pressed against his. He'd wanted her so much, but he'd known that it couldn't be. She'd only been seventeen. He'd been twenty-four.

But how he'd wanted her. Had loved her for as long as he could remember, but that feeling hadn't turned sexual until she turned fifteen. He'd known it wasn't right. Had chastised himself every night for the dreams he couldn't escape. He'd done his level best to get her out of his head. But no matter how many girls he dated, no matter how many he shared himself with, his feelings for Beth didn't change.

So he'd avoided her. Fortunately, whenever he visited after that one incident, she usually wasn't around since she'd gone off to medical school. Once or twice they'd run into each other during one of his brief visits with his mother. And then he'd heard that she was getting married and he'd decided that was good. With her married to someone else he could get on with his life instead of waiting for her.

Zach closed his eyes and shook his head. He had been waiting for her to grow up and get her M.D. She'd apparently never forgiven him for turning her away that one time and the next thing he knew it was too late.

He thought about the way she'd felt in his arms when he hugged her only minutes ago...the way she'd looked at him. And he wondered if she still felt it, too?

He shook off that ridiculous idea. They were different people now. Just because his body didn't realize that fourteen years had passed since that kiss was no indication that things hadn't changed big time for Beth.

Evcrything was different now.

Zach touched the glass as if he could somehow reach out to the woman who had stolen his heart so very long ago.

But he couldn't change the past.

Chapter Two

A quick shower relieved Beth of the grit and sweat of working in the garden with her mom, but nothing she did the entire afternoon assuaged the fire building in her belly for Zach. She could not evict him from her head now any more than she had been able to from her heart all those years ago. He was always there, just around the next thought. And she did not want to think about him.

Beth sighed and smoothed her hands over her cotton-blend sheath. She surveyed her reflection in the oval full-length mirror and was pleased with what she saw. The pale lemony color of the fabric contrasted well with her tanned skin. She didn't bother braiding her shoulder-length hair, allowing it to remain loose, something she seldom did. The color, she noted, was streaked with more gold than usual after her summer of helping in the garden when not at the hospital. She had never been much on housework. The outdoors beckoned to her on every level. Her father had ingrained the love of nature and all it had to offer deeply within her. Though he'd been gone half her life, she still missed him.

Despite her most valiant efforts, Zach pushed into

her musings, shoving aside all else. Did he see that same little girl next door when he looked at her now? After all, it had been five years since they'd even seen each other. Or did he see her as the woman she had so wanted him to notice all those years ago? Beth shook her head and chased those questions from her thoughts. She didn't care what Zach thought. If it was up to her she'd send him packing and right back to that fancy agency in Chicago. What was it called? The Colby Agency—that was it.

Why did he have to stay two weeks anyway? The answer zinged a direct hit right between her eyes. Mrs. Ashton had probably called and told him of the trouble she and Beth's mother were having. Colleen most likely persuaded her one and only son to come to her rescue. Not that Beth could blame her, especially considering she'd had that minor heart attack. And since she had no other children, who else would she call? Still, Zach's visit sure put a cramp in Beth's style. It was selfish of her to feel that way, but she did.

No matter how hard she tried not to, everything she did and said during his stay would be weighed against what he thought and whether or not she might run into him whenever she set foot outside her door.

Just like fourteen years ago all over again. Why else would she be standing in front of this mirror now? She rarely spent more than a few seconds checking her appearance. She wasn't a makeup, big hairdo kind of girl. Never had been. No hair spray or curling irons could be found in her bathroom, and few cosmetics. That realization had her peering even closer at her face and hair. She'd had the same cut for years. Was it time for a change?

Beth squared her shoulders and glowered sternly at the suddenly insecure woman staring back at her. "You are an adult," she scolded. "Act like one."

With that reprimand ringing in her ears, she went in search of her mother. They needed some one-on-one time in neutral territory—away from the Ashton environment.

Beth had to know what was going on with Colleen and Helen. All she had to do was find a way to get them back together and she would be saved. Helen would insist on taking charge of the party planning and Beth would be off the hook with Zach. Avoiding him wouldn't be that difficult then.

Helen McCormick was busily peeling potatoes when Beth entered the kitchen. Lingering near the door, she watched her mother for a bit before speaking. At sixty-five, Helen was still an attractive woman. She'd stayed fit and kept a good attitude about growing older. Her hair was more gray now than blond, and she kept the long mane braided and coiled around the crown of her head just like she had since Beth was a child. She smiled. Her mother was a good woman, a hardworking one who enjoyed life and never took anything for granted.

That was the main draw between Helen and Colleen. Both had such a zest for life. Though their backgrounds differed greatly, from education to financial status, the two were so much alike it was astounding and yet, each woman was entirely different—unique in her own right. Beth had seen the two squabble from time to time, but never had she known them to stop speaking to each other.

It just wasn't natural.

Zacharius Ashton, Senior, had been very generous

to Helen in his will, for no other reason than to show his appreciation for her years of companionship to his wife. Not that the McCormicks had ever wanted for anything anyway. The cottage was Helen's until the day she died. Her salary had always been well above average for the services she rendered, as had been Beth's father's. No one could accuse the Ashtons of anything less than complete fairness.

The arrangement had worked like a charm for nearly half a century. What on earth could have changed a relationship that long-standing?

"Let's have dinner out tonight, Mom," Beth suggested hopefully, announcing her presence as she crossed the kitchen to stand beside her mother. "You've worked hard today, you need a break."

Helen didn't look up from her efficient paring. "Thanks, honey, but I've got my heart set on that potato soup your grandmother used to make."

Beth shrugged. All dressed up and no place to go. "What can I do then?" She reached for the drawer that held the aprons while mentally reviewing the ingredients they would need.

"You just run along," Helen said, still not looking up. "I need some more thinking time."

Beth closed the drawer and leaned one hip against the cabinet. "Mom, look at me." She folded her arms over her chest and waited. When her mother at last relented and turned her way, Beth continued, "I don't know what's going on here, but I wish you'd let me in on it. This whole situation's just too disturbing. I can see what an effect it's having on you, not to mention Mrs. Ashton."

Helen dropped the knife and the nearly naked potato into the sink and dried her hands on a towel. "I can't tell you,'' she said finally. She folded the towel neatly and put it on the counter, her gaze focused intently upon the ivy embellished terry cloth. ''This is between Colleen and me.''

Beth wasn't going to give up that easily. ''You said there was something that needed to be said.''

Helen's deep brown gaze, the one Beth had inherited, connected with hers. ''There is, but it's not so simple.''

Beth shook her head. ''I don't understand. What could possibly be so earthshaking that you're afraid to say it out loud?''

Helen looked away, but not before Beth saw the truth of her own words. Her breath trapped in her chest. It was earthshaking. Whatever *it* was, it was big. The fear and pain she saw in her mother's eyes in that millisecond before she turned away made Beth's heart skip a beat.

''Okay.'' Beth swallowed at the lump of worry forming in her throat. This was definitely not good. ''We don't have to talk about it right now. I'm sorry. I shouldn't have brought it up. You and Colleen have been friends forever, you'll work it out in your own time.''

Her hands braced against the counter, Helen merely stared into the bowl of potatoes she'd been peeling.

Beth started to apologize again but the ringing of the telephone interrupted her. She sighed, walked to the back door and snagged up the receiver from the old beige rotary base hanging on the wall. She managed a pleasant hello.

''Miss Beth?''

"Yes." She frowned. The male voice sounded like—

"Mayor Chadwick here," he said in that aristocratic, take-charge air that was more than a few decibels too loud.

"How are you this evening, Mayor?" God, Beth hoped he wanted to speak to her mother. The man could talk for hours without saying anything at all.

"I'm fine, darlin', and you?"

"Couldn't be better," Beth lied through her teeth.

"The council and I are meeting at the diner tonight to organize our part of Ms. Colleen's celebration. Seeing as you're in charge of the planning now, we thought you might want to join us."

Beth tamped down the groan that welled in her chest. "What time?" She glanced at her watch. It was six now.

"Six-thirty all right with you? Josie's got chicken-fried steak on the blue plate special tonight." He chuckled. "The best chicken-fried steak in the whole county, you know."

Just what she needed, a plateful of cholesterol and an earful of bull. "Sure," Beth agreed, wincing inwardly at what lay before her. "I'll be there."

"I've already called Zach. He's coming, too."

Beth's jaw fell slack. The mayor said his goodbye and hung up before she could rally a verbal response. This couldn't be happening already. She needed a little more time to prepare. To brace herself against Zach's vast and varied charms.

Replacing the receiver, she turned back to her mother. Maybe she could talk Helen in to going with her. Beth was desperate.

"That was the mayor. He's asked me to meet with

the council to discuss Mrs. Ashton's birthday. Why don't you come with me, Mom?''

Her mother hesitated in her work, then slowly turned toward Beth. When their gazes locked the bright sheen of tears in her mother's eyes startled Beth. Helen McCormick never cried. She was too strong. The only time in her entire life that Beth had ever seen her cry was after her father's funeral.

"Please, let me help," Beth urged gently. "Whatever is wrong can't possibly be that bad."

"No matter what happens," her mother said, her voice trembling, "you remember that I love you more than anything in this world."

"Mother—"

Helen shook her head. "Run along." She resumed her potato peeling. "I don't want to talk about this anymore."

FEELING SORELY out of sorts, Zach settled into the driver's seat of his car and drove around to the McCormick's home. Mayor Chadwick had mentioned inviting Beth to this dinner meeting. Since her car was still here it seemed reasonable that she hadn't left yet. It also seemed reasonable for them to ride together. No point in driving two vehicles. It was definitely more economical to ride together, he concluded. And the time would give them a chance to discuss what was going on between their mothers.

As if either one of those excuses was his real motivation.

The truth was, he wanted to have a few minutes alone with her. It was that simple, and at the same time too complicated for him to understand completely.

Shutting off the engine, he pushed that admission away. It wouldn't be neighborly of him not to ask her if she wanted a ride. Zach smiled as he got out of the car and started for the door. That's right. This wasn't the city. People still went out of their way to help their neighbor down here. His gesture wouldn't be perceived as anything else. He certainly didn't want Beth to get the wrong idea.

Not that he had the right idea. He had no clue what was going on inside his head. His emotions were in a turmoil—as much from his mother's odd behavior as from his own. The whole situation was confusing. The one thing he was clear on was that his mother needed him, and he had to put all else aside. Especially these crazy urges where Beth was concerned.

Zach paused at the cottage's weathered door. He studied the arched portal, and then the ivy covered rock that surrounded it. The place had always seemed magical to him. Beth's father had been a wizard with plants and flowers. Her mother was always stirring something in a big pot and making the best cookies in the world. And Beth…well she was like the fairy princess who lived in the cottage. Who rehearsed her pirouettes in the moonlight and somehow appeared wherever he was by daylight. Whether he was practicing football or writing a history paper, she was there asking questions, trying to help, distracting him, making him laugh. Making him love her.

You do not want to go there, he reminded himself.

Shaking off the past, Zach raised his fist to knock at the same time the door opened.

Beth made a little sound of surprise and pressed her hand to her throat. "*Oh.* Hello, Zach," she said in that throaty voice that reminded him all too much of just how grown-up little Beth was now.

Unable to check the impulse, his gaze immediately swept the rest of her and his heart rate reacted accordingly. The dress was a soft yellow, not too short, just a few inches above the knee, not exactly form-fitting, but not loose either. The neck didn't scoop nearly low enough. All in all it was just a plain dress designed for comfort. But it was perfect and sexy as hell on her. The color contrasted the fresh, healthy glow of her skin. The lack of makeup and the fall of her silky hair around her smooth cheeks made her look twenty-one instead of thirty-one.

Beth McCormick was beautiful.

He experienced the sudden, almost overpowering, urge to touch her. He immediately tucked his hands into his trouser pockets, nipping the impulse to reach out to her in the bud before it blossomed and embarrassed them both.

"Chadwick told me he'd called you," Zach said, thrusting his emotions to the back of his mind much the same way he did in the courtroom or in a tense negotiation. "I thought we could ride together."

Those dark eyes widened and she looked on the verge of turning him down. In fact, he decided, on further consideration of her expression, she looked stricken.

"Come on, Beth," he coaxed. "I don't bite. It's only a ride into town."

She still didn't look convinced. Irritation trickled through him, dominating the good sense he'd intended to maintain in her presence. What was the deal here? What did she think he was? The big bad wolf? She never used to be afraid of him. Maybe she was still mad at him for turning her down all those years ago. If she only knew just how much he'd wanted to...

"I planned to drive myself," she announced, squaring her shoulders and looking straight at him now with no fear or reservation.

He let go a put-upon sigh. It didn't have to be this way. "Look." He searched her eyes, determined to sway her decision. "Let's not make this about the past. We're both adults now."

Something shifted in her dark eyes. Some barely perceptible something he couldn't quite read.

"You're right," she said, stepping across the threshold and into the tiny space between him and the door. She closed it behind her and stared directly into his eyes, her own glittering with annoyance she made no effort to conceal now. "I'm glad you finally noticed."

With that crisp remark, she sidestepped and brushed past him, the brief contact making his body tighten, and leaving the vaguest scent of roses.

Perplexed, Zach did an about-face, angled his head and watched her stride toward his car. Those long legs covered the distance in no time at all, but not quickly enough to prevent the gentle sway of her hips from doing strange things to his ability to breathe.

Oh, yes. She was definitely all grown up now.

But she was still Beth, and he had to remember that. She wasn't like the women he usually dated. Beth was a forever kind of girl. He frowned at the thought of the ex-husband he'd never even officially met. But Zach didn't have to meet him to know he didn't like him. Anyone who had hurt Beth was his enemy.

Zach clenched his jaw and strode to the car where Beth waited. No matter how much he was attracted to her, he would never, ever take advantage of her. Beth meant too much to him. Even if a misguided need for revenge or an urge to prove she could seduce him started her thinking along those lines, he would not allow it to happen. He almost laughed at that. Wishful thinking on his part. There was no denying what he still felt. But…he would protect her just like he always had.

He would protect her from him.

"A PARADE?" Beth repeated, certain she couldn't have heard the mayor right. Mrs. Ashton's birthday celebration was turning into a three-ring circus.

"Yes," Chadwick enthused. "Why Ms. Colleen is our most distinguished citizen. This momentous occasion simply demands that we pull out all the stops."

"We want to make an official presentation, too," Harve Baker, deputy mayor, added. "Like the keys to the city, only better."

"You're sure that's not a bit much?" Zach suggested, speaking for the first time since the group had exchanged greetings and settled down to talk business.

Beth darted a stealthy look in his direction. She'd made sure when she arrived that she sat where he couldn't end up next to her. With the table full, Zach had slid into a nearby booth opposite the mayor. Reclining against the wall so as to face those seated at the table, Zach looked relaxed and too darned good-looking. The light blue shirt set off the sky-blue of his eyes. The fit of those navy slacks displayed the best male buns she'd ever seen, and, as a doctor, she'd seen a few.

"I don't think so at all," Viola, the only female member of the council, piped up. "We did the same thing for Bert Sacks after he got himself on the *Letterman* show. Why shouldn't we do it for Colleen?"

Beth struggled not to groan. She remembered all too well the parade for Bert. The only celebrity in town. Too bad his ticket to fame had been a musical cow. Though she hadn't lived here at the time, Beth had come home for a weekend visit to find the whole town celebrating Bert's claim to fame. She'd almost turned around and driven right back to Indianapolis. But she'd needed a break, more to escape her disintegrating relationship than to get away from work. The marriage had been doomed from the beginning.

She shifted in her chrome and red vinyl chair. She was getting off track. Beth shoved thoughts of Matt and divorce from her mind. She didn't have time to think about men, past or present, right now.

"Well, see here, Viola," the mayor was saying. "We certainly intend to do right by Ms. Colleen. Her parade will be every bit as big as Bert's was."

Viola and the other members of the council made agreeable sounds. Beth cringed. The school band, the Girl Scouts, the local civic clubs—everyone would get into the act. Anyone who'd ever been voted for and won anything in this town, from Miss Valentine to top hog caller, would want a place in line. Beth pressed her fingers to her temples and wished she were anywhere but here.

"You'd be good at that, don't you think, Beth?" Viola asked.

Startled at hearing her name, Beth jerked to attention. Heat warmed her cheeks. No way was she going to allow anyone—specifically Zach—to know she hadn't been paying attention. "Oh, sure," Beth agreed with no clue to what the woman had said. "That sounds great."

He was watching her, she realized, tensing instantly. The beginnings of a smile played at the corners of his mouth, drawing her attention there… making her want to taste those full lips.

"Heads up," a crisp feminine voice warned.

Beth snapped from the forbidden fantasy. The waitress was circling the table, plates balanced in both hands. Beth silently railed at herself. She had to pull herself together here. She couldn't keep acting like she was seventeen all over again. She had this *community* event to plan. And, more important, she had to find some way to get the truth out of her mother.

A white stoneware plate laden with glistening green beans and chicken-fried steak accompanied by creamed potatoes dark with thick gravy was plopped down before her. Beth felt the arteries of her heart narrowing already. She glanced around the table and wondered if she was the only one concerned with living a little longer. When her gaze collided with Zach's, he was still watching her, those blue eyes expectant and somehow knowing. That smile slid fully across his lips now and he scooped up a forkful of potatoes and popped them into his mouth, a blatant challenge.

Instantly, Beth regressed to the summer she'd been twelve and determined she could beat Zach at anything he did—including eating her mother's lemon meringue pie.

She hated lemon pie to this day. The mere sight of it made her stomach queasy.

Beth firmed her resolve and booted the past back where it belonged, in some rarely visited corner of her mind. Her good eating habits would not be undermined by Zach Ashton. "Excuse me," she said to the waitress efficiently making her way around the table. "I've changed my mind. I'd like a salad, please. Dressing on the side."

"I CAN'T BELIEVE you missed out on Josie's chicken-fried steak." Zach chuckled as he pulled out onto Main Street, headed in the direction of home. "It was awesome." He glanced at his silent passenger. She looked even more beautiful by moonlight. Forcing his gaze straight ahead, he blinked away her lingering image. He wasn't supposed to be thinking that way, but he couldn't get his body and mind to cooperate with each other.

"It's called being health-conscious," Beth explained pointedly. "You should try it. After all, you're not getting any younger."

A brow notched up his forehead and he stole another quick look in her direction. "Ouch," he returned. "Surely one evening of eating on the edge won't drive the final nail in my coffin." A frown furrowed across his brow. "When did you get so uptight about every little thing anyway?"

She waved him off. "Typical male thinking, Ashton," she said irritably. "You think because you play the occasional game of racquetball and pound out a few miles on the treadmill once or twice a week that you're immune to the effects of aging."

He couldn't believe this. Was she insinuating that

he was old? "What has my age got to do with any-thing?" he demanded, irritation gnawing its way through his composure. He ran a couple miles every single day. Did his time at the gym three times a week as well.

She flared her palms impatiently. "Games, Ashton," she snapped. "You're still playing your immature little games. You thought if you ate it, I would. Don't try to tell me you didn't throw down the gauntlet back there with that first forkful of potatoes. Remember the lemon pie? You were always trying to prove you were better because you were older and a boy."

"A boy?" He darted another look at his lovely, albeit confusing, passenger. A grin stretched across his face at her stiff posture. She was furious. At what, he couldn't be certain. Surely they could put the past behind them if that's what the problem was. "I thought we'd already established that we're both adults now."

She folded her arms firmly over her chest. "Well, at least one of us is."

He braked to a stop at a red light. Was she accusing him of being immature just because he'd eaten his steak and potatoes? He ignored that little voice that told him she was right about the challenge. It was instinct. Whenever he was around Beth, he tried his level best to treat her like one of the guys. It was the only way to protect himself from doing something completely stupid—like kissing her. The mere thought made his muscles harden, some more than others.

"Would you care to elaborate on that innuendo?" he prodded, determined to get to the bottom of her unreasonable behavior once and for all. His mother's peculiar conduct was more than enough to contend with. He and Beth could at least be civil to each other. "The burden of proof lies with the accuser," he added when she didn't answer.

Beth rolled her eyes and huffed. "Don't use your lawyer talk on me. You know exactly what I mean."

"You're saying that one of us isn't an adult. I just wondered from what basis you drew your conclusions."

She shifted to face him, one long shapely leg crossed over the other, and totally unaware that her dress had slid up a few more inches, showing off a little more tanned thigh. Zach's mouth parched as he sneaked a second look.

"Well, let's see," she began, ticking off the list on her fingers. "There's the cherry-red sports car and the *GQ* look." She shook her head as if what he had was terminal. "Not to mention the immortal male attitude."

He glared at her, his foot going automatically to the accelerator when the light turned green. "What about my car and the way I dress?" Ire sprouted inside him. Sure he had a little attitude, but what the heck? A guy couldn't survive in his profession without a pair of brass ones.

She lifted one shoulder in a shrug of indifference, or maybe disdain. "I think any man who feels the need to express his insecurities so literally when he hits middle-age is immature."

Middle-age? Insecurities? He arrowed a glower in her direction. "You think I bought this car because I feel insecure about being closer to forty than thirty?"

She pursed those lush lips and inclined her head in triumph. "Yes, I do."

Fury hurdled through him. He didn't bother slowing down for the next light that went from yellow to red before he passed under it.

"I am not," he said, enunciating each word slowly, precisely, "going through any midlife crisis. I bought this car because I liked it. And there's absolutely nothing wrong with my clothes." He turned onto Hunter Ridge Road. "Or with the occasional meal that includes more than leaves and twigs."

She smiled patiently, as if completely certain of her assessment. "You date a different woman every weekend. You don't have time for a social life through the week," she added, nailing down his personal life in two short sentences. "You tell yourself that there's plenty of time for marriage and children later. That legitimately explains your single status and leaves you free from having to commit."

He shook his head. How the hell did she know all that? "What is this? The amateur psychology hour?"

"Am I right?"

Oh, he saw now. This was a trick. She was baiting him to get the answers she wanted. *She* wanted to know about his personal life—his *sex* life.

"Am I *right?*" she repeated, adding extra emphasis to the last word.

"If you want to know how often I have sex, just ask. And besides, what would you call divorcing the man you supposedly loved after five years of commitment?" A four-way stop gave him the opportunity to look directly at her and wait for the answer to his pointed question.

Silence thundered for several excruciatingly long beats.

She wasn't going to say anything. The dim glow from the dash didn't allow him to read her eyes completely, but he could see that he'd done what he intended. He had ended what she started. Cut her off at the knees like any good attorney would do. The knowledge gave him no pleasure. In an abrupt epiphany he also realized what he'd given away with his heartless remark—he knew the ink wasn't even dry on her divorce papers yet. She would know he'd asked about it.

"I'd call it a mistake," she said finally, her chin quivering slightly.

He held her gaze, hard as that proved in light of the hurt he knew he'd wielded. He wanted to hold her and apologize profusely for what he'd said and whatever the jerk she'd married had done. Disappointment pooled in his gut when he considered her words further. She thought she'd made a mistake. And all this time he'd thought he'd been the one who made the mistake. But then, they weren't talking about the same mistake.

"The divorce or the marriage?" he asked quietly, unable to help himself from pursuing the subject. He had to know.

She wanted to lie. God, a part of her wanted so badly to deny the truth…to somehow explain it away as something other than a personal failure. The other part of her wanted to hit Zach for even asking.

"The marriage," she relented tightly. "It was a mistake. But we're still friends."

She saw the sympathy flicker in those blue eyes. She was so hopelessly pathetic. She faced front, turning away from what she no longer wanted to see, especially from Zach.

"Sorry," he said contritely. "I shouldn't have—"

"It's okay." She didn't want to hear what she'd already seen in his eyes.

"Are we through fighting?" he asked softly, too softly.

She continued her stare into the darkness. "I guess so."

"What are we going to do about our mothers?"

Beth closed her eyes. She didn't want to think about that either. "I don't know. I don't understand what's going on."

Zach pulled away from the intersection. "I can't figure it out. Something's changed though. Mom isn't behaving like her usual self."

At a loss to stop herself, Beth studied his handsome profile, her heart doing a little dance in spite of the anger she'd felt at him just moments ago. "Different how?" She wondered if it was anything like her own mother's odd behavior.

He exhaled noisily. "I can't exactly pinpoint it, just different. She told me she loved me three times in the space of as many minutes. She was almost clingy."

Beth knew exactly what he meant then. Colleen Ashton was one of the strongest women Beth knew, her mother included. Colleen had never been one to show her affection with outward gestures. Hers was always an understated way.

"Your mother won't tell you anything?" he asked as he parked and turned off the engine and lights, leaving nothing but the moon to relieve the darkness that now cloaked them.

"Nothing."

"We have to get to the bottom of this," he said, his voice curling around her in the still, dark night. "At their age life is too uncertain to stay mad at each other. Think how one would feel if something happened to the other while this standoff was going on."

Beth nodded. "What can we do?"

"Just keep plugging away until we figure out what it is that's caused this kind of damage."

At that moment Beth wanted more than anything in this world to feel Zach's arms around her. Further proof that nothing had changed. They could be yelling at each other one minute, then making up the next. "Good idea," she mumbled, then quickly scrambled out of the car. She would not let her emotions get the better of her again.

Zach followed her up the flagstone walk and to her door. She faced him there, the glow from the outside light pooling around them like a dim spotlight. Good-night would be said right here. She didn't want him to come inside. She'd had all the Zach stimuli she could handle for one night.

"Thanks for the ride," she said lamely. Truly pathetic.

"Any time," he offered in that deep, husky voice.

"Good night, Zach." The words sounded breathless. But how could they sound any other way with him standing so close and her pulse tripping so out of control? She wanted to back up but the closed door was right behind her, preventing her escape.

When his gaze dropped to her mouth the air evaporated from her lungs.

"Good night," he murmured.

Slowly, very slowly, he leaned toward her. Her

heart pounded so hard she was certain he could hear it. She moistened her lips, in anticipation of his sealing completely over hers.

But they didn't. Instead, he pressed that perfect mouth to her forehead.

As if she were a child.

Or his little sister.

"See you tomorrow." With one last breath-stealing smile, he turned and walked away.

She wanted to scream. Fury mushroomed inside her. She opened her mouth to tell him she would be busy tomorrow, but he suddenly stopped and faced her. She snapped her mouth shut.

"By the way," he said in that teasing tone that was all charm and Ashton, "I think it's great how you agreed to come up with the theme for the whole event."

Theme?

Grinning widely, Zach winked and strolled away.

Beth sagged against the old wooden door and watched him go. So that's what Viola had asked her. Beth mentally recited a few choice expletives. What did she know about themes? She was a doctor. She didn't do themes.

One way or another she had to mend this rift between her mother and Zach's. Her heart couldn't take spending this much one-on-one time with the only man she'd ever really loved...

...the same one who'd never thought of her as anything but the girl next door.

Chapter Three

Colleen Ashton signed the letter she'd just finished writing and made quick work of folding it, then tucked it into the matching embossed envelope. She sealed it, penned her son's name on the front, then set it aside to put in the safe when she finished the remainder of this morning's correspondence. She restrained the uncharacteristic tears that crowded her throat for the second time today.

No one would ever convince her that she was making a mistake. Not even Helen whom she trusted with her life.

The thought that she and Helen had not spoken in more than twenty-four hours weighed heavy on Colleen's heart. But there was nothing to be done about it. She and Helen didn't see eye to eye on the matter and she doubted that anything was going to change that indisputable fact.

"We have a problem."

Colleen's head came up at the unexpected sound of Helen's voice. As Helen crossed the room, Colleen stood, squared her shoulders and faced what would likely be another attempt to sway her decision.

But she would not relent. It was completely out of the question.

"I thought we weren't speaking," Colleen said crisply when her friend paused next to the antique writing desk.

Helen raised one tawny brow. "We aren't, but this is an emergency."

"What sort of emergency?"

It irritated Helen to no end that Colleen could be so blasted analytical about everything—including this. Helen wanted to shake some sense into her, but she knew Colleen too well. Nothing would change her mind unless she wanted to change it. Unfortunately, she didn't.

"Beth suspects something."

Colleen wasn't the least bit surprised. "I would imagine she does. After that little performance you gave in here yesterday, I would think the whole world suspects something is amiss."

"No."

The singular word spoken so sharply echoed in the room. Fear seeped into Colleen's weary bones.

"I mean she *really* suspects. I'm sure she's talked to Zach already."

Colleen nodded. "She has. Zach gave me the third degree last night after he returned from town."

"It's time," Helen said, her gaze pinning Colleen's with fierce determination. "What if you'd died when you suffered that heart attack? I can't take this secret to the grave with me. I just can't do it."

"But I didn't die." Colleen lifted her chin a notch. "It wouldn't have changed anything if I had. We both know that."

"It's wrong for us to say nothing," Helen insisted,

her expression as grim and desperate as her tone. "You know it's wrong."

"If that's all you have to say then there's nothing else to discuss." Colleen held her ground, not giving an inch. "You and Beth are a part of this family, Helen. As much as you mean to me, I will not allow you to take matters into your own hands. We took an oath never to speak of this again."

"We were young." Helen shook her head, tears shining in her worried eyes. "We didn't think."

Colleen struggled to hold back her own tears. "Helen McCormick, I will hold you to that oath until the day I die."

Helen swiped at the lone tear that managed to escape her brutal hold on her emotions. "This is wrong and you know it. It's a mistake."

"That may be. But it's my decision. If it's a mistake, then it's mine to make."

Two long beats passed before Helen walked away.

Colleen watched her go, sadness welling inside her. What was done was done. There was no turning back now.

"YOU'RE SURE you want to tackle this job, Mr. Ashton?"

Hank, the local handyman, eyed Zach speculatively. At sixty, the man had attempted just about any kind of fixer-up job one could imagine. Including getting his portly frame trapped under Widow Murphy's house while repairing her faulty plumbing. Ten at the time, Zach vividly recalled the local volunteer fire department having to rescue the man. He doubted Hank crawled under many houses these days. But he'd kept up the maintenance here ever since Beth's father died.

Zach turned his attention back to the ornate gazebo nestled amid the lush landscape of the backyard where he'd played as a child. Since his mother had decided to have her birthday party here, the gazebo, she had insisted, required a fresh coat of paint. It looked fine to Zach, but then he wasn't a painter. And it wasn't his birthday. Whatever his mother wanted, he intended to make sure she got.

"You know," Zach began somewhat hesitantly, "I think I will do it myself." At least this way he'd have something to do besides think about the one thing he'd sworn he wouldn't.

Hank stroked his jaw and studied the large structure as if assessing the possibility. "You'll need the right equipment. Ladders, brushes and such."

Zach nodded, his gaze shifting to the other man. "You could take care of that for me, couldn't you?"

"Sure. Be happy to. I'll set you up right now, if you'd like. I can even run down to the hardware and pick up the paint." Hank smoothed a stubby hand over one intricately carved post. "A nice semigloss would be your best bet."

Never one to waste time once he'd made a decision, Zach said, "Let's do it then."

Hank adjusted his cap, then hung his thumbs on the suspenders of his overalls. "I'll have everything set up within the hour."

"Excellent. I'll be ready."

The handyman lumbered off in the direction of his truck. Zach watched him drive away, then walked slowly toward the French doors at the back of the house. He hadn't slept more than an hour last night.

And there was no one to blame but himself. He'd known when he came here the risk involved if Beth happened to visit at the same time. Not to mention the infernal restlessness that always plagued him. He was a man of action. He wasn't one to sit around waiting for things to happen. Finding something tangible to occupy his time would alleviate the latter problem, but Beth was another story.

The last thing he'd expected to find was her living here again. Zach rubbed the back of his neck, the move proving useless in his attempt to loosen too-tense muscles. She was divorced and sharing her childhood home with her mother. He resisted the urge to glance in the direction of the cottage. She wasn't there anyway. She'd left early that morning, probably for the hospital. He'd watched from his bedroom window. The same way he'd watched her every move back when he'd lived at home, or on the occasions he'd visited after leaving for law school.

He'd had it all planned out in his mind sixteen years ago. Beth was too young for him, way too young. He knew how important it was to her mother that she got her education. How important it would be to Beth. Helen McCormick wanted better for her only child than she'd had herself. All parents wanted that, he supposed. Zach's own mother was no exception. She, in typical Colleen fashion, had ensured Beth's attendance at one of the top medical schools in the nation by calling the Dean personally. As a high school graduation present, Colleen had given Beth a check that would, combined with Helen's savings, pay Beth's tuition in full. Beth and Helen had adamantly objected, but there was no changing an Ashton's mind once it had been made up.

The McCormicks weren't just employees. They were family. And Zach'd had plans for the youngest McCormick. All he'd had to do was be patient. He'd carefully maintained a safe distance, as difficult as that had proven. Especially after Beth hit junior high. She'd made no secret of her feelings for him. He'd read how much she loved him in those big dark eyes way before she'd ever said the words out loud or kissed him. He had known that if he let his guard down it would be a mistake. He would have wanted more than that kiss…had wanted more. One thing would have led to another and he couldn't allow that to happen until Beth was old enough to know whether she wanted to spend the rest of her life with him. He didn't want her making a lifetime commitment until she fully understood what it entailed. Her happiness meant too much to him.

So he'd been the refined gentleman his mother and father had raised him to be, and he'd waited.

The day she graduated from medical school he had intended to tell her how he felt. She would forgive him then, he'd been certain, for turning her away all those years ago. She would understand that he'd been right all along. That he'd had her best interests at heart. Both had needed to be sure of what they wanted before taking such a life-altering step, like marriage. But when he arrived on graduation day, flowers and ring in hand, she was already engaged to someone else. So he'd just walked away. Beth hadn't even known he was there. It was his fault after all. He should have gone to her sooner and explained his feelings. Instead, he'd stayed away. Too busy building his career and proving he could be everything his father had believed he could. He'd finally achieved the success he'd sought so fiercely when Victoria Colby had made him an offer. He'd been ready then to get married and start a family.

But all of those dreams had died an instant death when he'd seen Beth in the arms of another man. Zach paused to steady his shaky composure before going inside the house. He'd put all that behind him years ago. He couldn't understand why he was putting himself through it all over again now. It wasn't like he hadn't had other women. He'd gone through dozens while waiting for the only one he wanted. But he'd waited too long.

Zach dismissed the past from his mind. None of that mattered now. He was here for his mother, not for Beth. It was good to see her, but whatever had been between them was over...the opportunity had passed.

He clenched his jaw at the memory of how touching her, of simply pressing his lips to her forehead just last night had affected him. He still wanted her desperately, at least on a physical level. His gut instinct told him that she was still attracted to him as well. He doubted it would take much on either of their parts to fall into a brief affair. A two-week affair to be exact. He shook his head. He wouldn't do that. He was used to short relationships, but Beth wasn't. He wouldn't risk hurting her that way. It wasn't her fault he'd screwed up.

Their lives were different now. There was no going back. That time had passed. Zach didn't want those things anymore. He had no desire for marriage and family. He'd banished those concepts from his life the day Beth married another man. He'd gotten used to being a confirmed bachelor. The fact of the matter was he enjoyed playing the field. What did he need with a permanent relationship at this point in his life? He spent far too many hours at the office to be a good husband or father. He was probably too old to change.

But he and Beth could have what they'd always had—friendship. He would walk on broken glass to protect that precious bond. No matter how attracted they were to one another, he wouldn't risk hurting Beth again.

Zach opened the door and stepped into the house. The summer room was quiet and deserted. It had never been that way back in his days as a teenager. He studied the way the sunlight streamed in through the numerous windows warming the comfortable overstuffed furnishings and nurturing the entourage of plants and indoor trees. The only room in the house that contained a television set, this had been Zach's favorite. He and his buddies had spent many fall Saturday afternoons watching college football in here. He and Beth had spent just as many Saturday nights watching movies in here, too. They'd stretched out on the carpet and shared a big bowl of popcorn. He smiled at the protective feeling that welled in him even now. Later, when he'd had the occasional weekend home from college, his feelings had changed. He remembered the first time he'd looked at Beth and felt something different... something that startled him.

Zach swore hotly at himself, using a particularly nasty compound adjective that described perfectly his inability to keep his head on straight. He needed to focus on the problem at hand. His mother.

"Shame on you, Zacharius Ashton," Colleen

scolded. "Where on earth did you learn such language?"

Speak of the devil. She crossed the room with slow, measured steps, her gaze searching his. "At law school," he lied, putting his disturbing predicament aside for the moment. He leaned down and pressed a kiss to her waiting cheek. "It was required methodology for closed door negotiations."

His mother smiled fondly as she caressed his jaw with one frail hand. "You're so like your father. Confident, strong and so handsome."

Zach smiled, too, remembering. "But he always told me that I got my blue eyes from the milkman."

Colleen patted his shoulder. "The broad shoulders, too," she mused, going along with the old family joke. "That milkman was a real looker."

Zach took her hand in his and ushered her toward the sofa. "Sit with me for a while." Hank wouldn't be back with the paint for another half hour or so, there was time.

Colleen settled primly on the edge of the sofa, the pink of her tailored suit enhancing the light dusting of blush on her pale cheeks. "Did you talk to Hank about freshening up the gazebo?"

Zach sat down next to his mother and stretched out his long legs. "I did." He crossed his legs at the ankles. "But I decided to paint it myself."

Colleen looked aghast. "You can't be serious. Why you've never painted anything in your life. You might…" She waved a hand fretfully. "You might fall off the ladder and break something important."

He laughed. "Well, hopefully I won't break anything—important or not."

She frowned and assessed him more closely. He

couldn't be sure if it was out of concern or if she feared the damage he might do to her gazebo or the surrounding shrubbery.

"I'm sure Hank would be happy to do the job."

"He's going to help," Zach assured her. "Don't worry, I won't make a mess."

Knowing him far too well to pursue the issue, she patted his hand. "I'm confident you'll do a fine job. We'll tell everyone at the party that you painted it yourself."

"You'd better wait to see how it turns out before you corner bragging rights," he said with a chuckle. "Speaking of the party, I really think Beth and I need Helen's input on some things. Any chance you might talk her into helping us out?"

Colleen's expression closed instantly. "I'm sure you'll do fine on your own." As if he'd pushed her personal eject button, she shot straight to her feet. "I should see what cook has on the menu for dinner tonight."

He snagged her hand and halted her hasty departure. Zach shook his head. "Let's talk a little more." She reluctantly allowed him to draw her back down to the sofa but she wouldn't look at him. "Come on, Mom, this is ridiculous. Why don't you tell me what's going on between you and Helen?"

"There's nothing to talk about. We simply don't see eye to eye on a particular issue that I refuse to discuss with you or anyone else. The case is closed."

Zach held her hand in his. "That sounds a little final," he said softly. "Are you sure you want to leave it that way? What if something happened…?"

Colleen lifted an aristocratic eyebrow and glared at him. "Then it'll be on her head," she said sternly.

"This is her choice not mine. I never go back on my word."

Surprised, a frown pulled his lips downward. He'd never heard his mother speak so strongly against her good friend. "Surely there's some way to resolve the issue."

His mother pulled her hand free of his and stood once more. "There isn't. Now—" she stepped out of his reach "—if you'll excuse me, I have things to see to."

There was nothing he could do but let her go. She was an Ashton. Unless she decided to change her mind, which wasn't likely, then the only hope lay with Helen. As soon as Beth came home they would have to talk. There had to be a way to get Helen to come clean on the issue. Frustrated, Zach fell back against the sofa. That, he thought, disconcerted, would mean spending more time with Beth and fighting feelings he didn't want to feel…fantasizing about things he knew could never be.

But he had to do it. He would simply find a way to be with her without losing control. He was an Ashton after all.

BETH STARED at the report lying on her desk. She closed her eyes and shook her head, defeat weighing heavy on her heart. Leukemia. The aggressive, ugly kind. Couldn't it have been anything else?

Beth opened her eyes and reread the report once more. Her patient, Laurie Ellroy, would definitely die without proper treatment. There was no two ways about it. Oh, the oncologist would try chemo, but the chances of it working alone were so minimal that they weren't even worth mentioning. To cure her it would take massive doses of the meanest chemo available, and then Laurie would still die without a bone-marrow transplant. Her mother's own health problems prevented her from being a donor. Her father was dead and she had no brothers and sisters. They could look for a match elsewhere, but the chances were slim that they would find a suitable one.

Laurie, twenty-two years old, fresh out of college with a degree in education, was going to die.

Beth's lips trembled. She bit her lower one to stop the quivering. She didn't want Laurie to die. Her life had just begun. She was engaged to her high school sweetheart. God, it just wasn't fair. Beth scrubbed at a tear that managed to escape her firm hold on her emotions. This was the part she hated about practicing medicine. The cases where her hands were tied. When she'd referred Laurie to the internist, she'd hoped he would find something fixable. But he hadn't. And the oncologist's prognosis was less than optimistic.

Laurie's mother was devastated. Beth couldn't even imagine the horror of losing a child. She thought of her own mother. They were so close, how would either of them survive the loss of the other? Losing her father had been agonizing, but she and her mother had clung to each other until the hurt subsided to a tolerable level. And Zach had been there for her, just like she'd been there for him when his father died. They were family. But if Beth lost her mother, she would be completely alone. She couldn't turn to Zach now like she had back then. It wasn't the same anymore.

Last night plowed its way into her mind. Beth

tamped down the anger that wanted to well in her chest. Zach Ashton was the most confusing, frustrating man she had ever known. On one hand, he made her want to scream at him, or maybe even hit him. And on the other, she wanted nothing more than to go straight into his arms and stay right there.

She huffed a breath of frustration. How could she still want him so after what he'd done to her? He'd tossed her aside, seeing nothing but the little girl next door. He'd been too busy with the more sophisticated, older women he'd met in college and then his career. The memory of how naive she'd been at seventeen still infuriated her. She was supposed to forget about him. But she simply couldn't. And God knows she'd tried.

Case in point, Matt Daniels. She'd decided the night before med school graduation that she would take him up on his proposal. He'd asked her three times and seemed crazy about her. He was nice-looking, and they shared a love of healing. What did she have to lose? Zach obviously wasn't interested and she was tired of waiting. She'd certainly mooned over him long enough. Of course Matt wasn't the first man she'd dated in an effort to erase Zach's indelible imprint from her memory. There'd been a few others, none of which stuck or made enough of an impact to evict Ashton from her heart.

Beth pushed away from her desk. It was after five o'clock, she was tired and there was nothing else she could do here. Though the thought of going home held no real appeal considering she would no doubt run into Zach. Then again, how could she avoid him when they had this darned party to coordinate? *The theme.* She had that stupid theme to come up with.

Beth massaged her forehead with her thumb and forefinger. How did one come up with a theme for this sort of thing?

She dug the telephone book from beneath the mountain of papers on her desk and flipped to the Yellow Pages. "*P*," she muttered. "Painters, paneling, parties." Beth dragged her finger down the listing until she found what she wanted. *The Party Store*. Surely they would have suggestions either on display or in a book. She grabbed her purse and decided it was definitely time to call it a day. She could stop at The Party Store on the way home. And if she were lucky, she could nail down this theme in one stop.

Before leaving, Beth called her mom and told her that she was making a couple of stops before coming home. Helen worried if Beth didn't make it home on time. Beth smiled wryly. At least someone worried. Zach's image flitted through her weary mind. She doubted he ever worried about anything other than his next case. Knowing that little accusation was completely unfounded, but feeling immensely better at thinking about him in any way other than sexual, she didn't immediately dismiss it. She needed to concentrate on all the reasons she could not keep up this ridiculous infatuation of the man.

She was tired of all the Zach worship. He was just a man. She stilled, her hand on the knob of her office door. Why hadn't she really looked at him and realized that fact all these years? Sure he was good-looking and smart. Built, and probably hung, a wicked little voice added. Beth slipped out, locked her office door and hurried down the corridor as she pondered that line of thinking further. He was just a guy she'd lived next door to her whole life and she'd gotten infatuated with him. If they had ever followed through on her teenage desires, she'd probably have found that there was nothing particularly special about him and moved on. Beth slowed as she exited the hospital. Would getting him out of her system be that simple?

What had kept her from thinking of this before? A smile spread across her lips. The only thing that made Zach so godlike in her mind was his being just out of her reach. All she had to do was have him just one time and she'd know there was nothing special about him. The mystery would be unveiled. The tension broken. Kind of like Christmas as a kid. All that obsessing for months before it arrived, then—*bam*— it's over.

"Well, hell." She stood in the middle of the staff parking lot, her hands planted on her hips. All this time she'd thought he was something special when he really wasn't. He was just a regular guy. She'd built him into some kind of Adonis in her mind because he'd always stood up for her, been kind to her. And she'd never be free of that long-standing perception unless she proved to herself once and for all that it was just that—a perception.

Anticipation tingled through her. Could it be that easy?

There was only one way to find out.

Now all she had to do was convince Zach to go along with her plan. A scowl tugged her features into a frown. He would never do it. They were friends, he'd insist. She thought of last night's infuriatingly platonic kiss. She was like a sister to him. The little girl next door. But she was all grown up now. A grin tilted her lips upward. She wouldn't play by Zach's rules. She was going to be in control of this game.

And seduction was its name.

THE PARTY STORE carried a huge selection of birthday themes—none of which reached out to Beth. None said "Colleen Ashton." Beth shifted her purse to the other shoulder and retraced her path down the only aisle that even remotely interested her. A vague possibility for the theme was forming in the back of her mind.

With her elbow propped on one arm she rested her chin in her hand and sighed with disgust. Why the heck did they need a theme anyway? Couldn't they just do it? All they really needed was a nice cake and a rousing rendition of "Happy Birthday." A smile tugged at her lips. And she knew just who could do it.

"Decisions, decisions," a decidedly male voice murmured right next to her ear.

Beth shrieked and jumped away from the sound. Deep, rich laughter sent her fright rushing toward anger. She whipped around to find Zach grinning at her. The urge to stamp her foot was almost overpowering.

"What are you doing here?" she demanded instead.

He smoothed a hand over his mouth, obviously to hide his infuriating grin, and cocked his head at her. "Your mother said you were here, I thought you might need my help," he offered, amusement still lingering in his voice.

Beth adopted an offended expression. "I'm doing quite well on my own, thank you."

He stared at her empty hands, then arched a skeptical eyebrow. "I can see that. I suppose that's why you haven't picked out anything yet."

She struggled to maintain her irritation at a level that would not give him the satisfaction she was certain he would feel at knowing he'd annoyed her. "I'm only looking today. I'll need more time to consider all the possibilities."

That lopsided grin that stole her breath spread across his handsome face again. "You don't have a clue what you're going to do. Truth be told, you'd rather eat lemon meringue pie than be responsible for selecting this theme."

The fury that welled in her chest made a deep breath impossible. "If you're not going to offer helpful suggestions, why did you bother coming all the way to Cartersville?"

He shrugged nonchalantly. "Actually, I needed to leave the car at the shop for maintenance and I thought maybe you'd give me a lift back home."

Now she was his chauffeur. Just what she needed, twenty minutes alone in the car with him without proper preparation. "Fine," she said tightly. "I'm almost finished here."

He nodded once. "Great."

For the first time since he'd scared the wits out of her by sneaking up behind her she looked at him. Really looked at him. He was wearing criminally faded jeans with white paint splotches on them and a worn black T-shirt with even more paint splatters on it. But the ancient material hugged his muscular body like he'd just walked out of a tailor's shop. Her pulse reacted. Beth forced her gaze above his awesome chest and looked directly at his face, which only made matters worse. There was even a speck of paint on his left cheek. She blinked, trying to dispel the incredibly sexy image.

"I was painting the gazebo," he said as if he'd read her mind and needed to explain his unpolished appearance. He was clearly out of his element without his Armani. "I had to drop everything and rush over here to catch the mechanic otherwise he wouldn't have any time available while I'm here. He's the best, you know."

The image of Zach on a ladder, his muscles flexing and contracting with every stroke of the brush loomed large in her mind. Her mouth went dry, and her heart did a funny little flip-flop. Now was as good a time as any to put her plan into action, she decided, her body all too ready to begin. And begin she did. She allowed her gaze to linger on his face, relearning every angle…every chiseled masculine feature. And that mouth. Another flip-flop in her chest. His lips were full, but not feminine. The hint of those wicked dimples was present even when he wasn't smiling…like now. And the eyes…those blue bedroom eyes. So intent…so alluring. She never made it to the hair. She just couldn't take her gaze from his.

"I'm…you're not making this easy," he murmured hesitantly.

She watched his lips move when he spoke. He was speaking to her she knew, but at the moment what he said didn't seem to matter. All that mattered was the heat and desire buzzing between them. It was there. She could feel it. He could feel it, too. She saw it in his eyes, heard it in his voice.

"Beth, are you all right?"

She dragged her gaze from that tempting mouth

and looked directly into his eyes. "No," she said in all honesty. "I'm not sure I'll ever be all right again if I don't do this."

She kissed him. Just reached right up, grabbed him by the ears and pulled his mouth down to hers.

He resisted at first, his mouth hard, unyielding. But within seconds he'd given in to the kiss. She threaded her fingers into his thick hair and kissed him harder still. She traced the seam of his lips and, without reservation, he opened. Her tongue slid inside his mouth and his taste filled her. Sweet and citrusy, like lemonade, yet hot and demanding.

His arms went around her waist and pulled her close. She almost moaned at the feel of his lean, muscular body against hers. Oh, how she had wanted this…wanted it for so very long. Her heart stumbled when he took control of the kiss. She could taste his sudden desperation…could sense the yearning for more. And she wanted more, too. She leaned fully into him. He groaned, or maybe she did. The sound was lost between them. She could feel his body hardening with the inferno they were creating one hot, licking flame at a time. The nudge of his arousal made her burn to know him completely, intimately.

He dragged his mouth from hers, his breathing as unstable as her own. He stared down at her lips as if he might just devour them all over again, then that hooded gaze connected with hers. She saw the confusion that battled with the same fierce need she felt.

"Well," he rasped, his voice thick with desire. "That was…interesting."

She smiled seductively, her gaze never deviating from his. "That—" she traced his bottom lip with one fingertip, then licked the taste of him from her own lips "—was only the beginning."

Chapter Four

Twenty minutes in the shower under a cool spray of water had washed away all signs of Zach's afternoon of working up a healthy sweat scraping and painting the gazebo, but it had done nothing at all to alleviate the other kind of heat slowly building inside him. He braced his hands against the tiled wall and turned his face up to the water's spray. Thoughts of touching...kissing Beth played over and over inside his head. He wanted her. He wanted her desperately. The need twisted inside him, a pleasure-pain.

Zach pressed his forehead against the cool tile and swore at his own stupidity. He knew better than this. Beth wasn't some one-night stand. She wasn't the sort of woman a guy took to bed because he felt the urge to have sex. She was the kind a guy married. And, dammit, he wasn't the marrying kind anymore. He was past all that.

Besides, she wouldn't want him anyway. She'd been married once already. And she'd chosen a guy her age...a guy who shared her professional interests. A guy completely different from him. Zach gritted his teeth and suppressed the urge to hit something...like the fool who'd broken Beth's heart.

The other one. The one she'd married.

He'd been the first to hurt her. Zach straightened and shoved the wet hair from his face. He'd been too full of himself to realize just how much he'd hurt her until it was too late. The idea that maybe he had a second chance now flitted through his mind. He pushed that notion away without hesitation. Too much had happened...they were different people now. According to his mother, Beth hadn't cared for city life. He supposed that was true since she'd chosen to return to her small-town home after her divorce. And Zach couldn't live anywhere else. The city was his life. Well, that and the Colby Agency. He lived for his work. It defined him. It always had.

He gave the brass knob a twist, turning off the water, then grabbed a thick white towel and made a half-hearted effort at drying. It was his number one character flaw—extreme ambition. He'd inherited the fierce, undeniable trait from his mother. Nothing got in his way when he focused on a goal. He never, ever failed to achieve what he set out to obtain. Except, he amended as he slung the towel haphazardly around his waist, that once.

He'd royally screwed up where Beth was concerned. Raking his hair back with his fingers, he stared at his reflection in the mirror and suddenly felt old. He flattened his palms on the cool porcelain of the pedestal sink and steadied himself against the weight of his past. Regret was a waste of time. He rarely allowed himself to experience the emotion. But that didn't stop him now. He closed his eyes and considered for just one moment what could have been.

If he'd handled things differently, he and Beth

might be married now. Maybe they'd even have kids. That thought made his gut clench. *Married…kids.* He told himself every day that he didn't care about those things, but it was a lie. He just didn't want them with anyone else.

Zach sighed and opened his eyes to stare at his reflection once more. That time had passed. He accepted that reality. Whatever Beth wanted right now, it wasn't him…not like that anyway. Maybe it was payback for the way he'd ignored her all those years. Maybe she just needed to prove to herself that she could make him want her. He frowned as he considered that logic for the second time since seeing her.

Here he was berating himself for even thinking about taking advantage of Beth in that way and just maybe she was the one who wanted to take advantage of him…in a manner of speaking. This could be about nothing more than revenge. She knew he was only in town for a couple of weeks. Maybe she wanted to find out what it would be like…

…what *they* would be like. *Together.*

He had to remember that Beth wasn't a kid anymore. She was a woman. The image of her soft curves and voluptuous mouth filled his head. A fully grown, very beautiful woman. One who was no longer a virgin…no longer a naive schoolgirl who lived next door and tempted him beyond all reason.

But she'd married someone else. The niggling of anger that always accompanied that thought poked him now. She hadn't wanted him. What the hell made him think she wanted him now…for anything other than recreational sex?

"You're a mess, pal." Zach shoved away from the sink and walked into his dimly lit room. He flipped on the overhead light and contemplated what the hell he was going to do now. It would be dark in an hour or so. His mother was going out with a friend for the evening. He had to do something to get his mind off Beth or sex…or both. A strange restless feeling nagged at him relentlessly. A near constant state of arousal was driving him insane. He needed relief.

He considered for about two seconds going into town to check out the nightlife, but quickly nixed that possibility. There wouldn't be that much night-life to check out and, besides, anyone he ran into would know his mother if not him. The fact that he was still a bachelor had not escaped the local single ladies. The last thing he wanted was a steady stream of husband-prospectors dropping by. And they would. He wasn't blind. He was a pretty good-looking guy and he'd stayed in shape. He had a pres-tigious job. But it would be the Ashton name that attracted the ladies hereabouts. And he was no glut-ton for punishment, nor was he the kind of guy who would take advantage of a woman who hoped to ne-gotiate herself a marriage proposal.

That left one choice as far as alleviating his phys-ical condition. He would just have to work it off. He hadn't worked out, other than the painting, since he arrived. A nice, long run would take care of his prob-lem. At least temporarily.

"Why didn't you think of this before, Ashton?" he muttered as he prowled through drawers in search of suitable running attire. He'd do a few miles hard and fast, then a few more a little slower. By the time he stumbled back to his room he'd be way too exhausted to think about sex.

Or Beth.

BETH TIED her running shoes and stood. She glanced around her room and almost sighed at all she had to do. Her laundry was knee-deep. She'd brought home a half-dozen reports she needed to review. The files and the palm-size recorder she used for dictating lay waiting on her bed. And she still didn't have the darned theme for Mrs. Ashton's birthday celebration ironed out. The mayor would be hounding her about that in a day or two. But right now, she had to get out of here. Had to run off some of this adrenaline.

Promising herself she would take care of the reports and the laundry before she went to bed, she started her warm-up routine. She stretched her upper body first, then spent twice as long stretching out her leg muscles. Two or three miles would do her good in more ways than one.

She had to gather her perspective on the Ellroy case. She was a professional; she couldn't allow this case or any other to become so personal. But it hurt to watch the young woman's life hang so precariously in the balance. If a donor wasn't found, she would certainly die.

The fact was Laurie Ellroy was no longer Beth's concern, medically speaking. An oncologist had taken over the case, an excellent doctor who Beth respected. But Mrs. Ellroy remained adamant that Beth was to stay involved. Truth be told, she wanted to be involved. This case—the people involved in this case—meant a great deal to her.

Beth banished those thoughts, took a deep breath and bent at the waist. She wrapped her fingers around her left ankle and extended in that direction as far as she could and held, stretching out her hamstrings. She would not think of work for the next hour. She would run until she was spent, then she would take a long, leisurely soak in the tub.

And think about Zach.

She straightened and shook off that last thought. She would not think about Zach. She'd behaved rashly this afternoon. She'd fully intended to set her plan into motion but at a more appropriate time and place. Zach had been shocked by her actions. He'd talked incessantly the entire drive home, about everything from the weather to the price of gasoline. It had been painful to listen to. He clearly did not want to pursue the issue or her.

Nothing had changed.

Tamping down the urge to throw something, she caught her hair in one hand and tucked it quickly into a serviceable ponytail. Maybe nothing had changed, but that didn't mean change wasn't possible. On a mental level he might not want to be seduced by Beth. He might even still see her as the kid next door, but on a physical level he'd been more than ready. She'd felt every hard inch of the evidence he could not deny.

But did she want it to be that way?

Was she really ready to chase Zach Ashton again?

She glared out her bedroom window and in the direction of his, the way she'd done a thousand times as an infatuated adolescent. As if she'd somehow summoned him he stepped into view. Without thought she moved to the window, leaned against the bureau there and reluctantly took in the whole picture. She wanted to ignore the rows of lush roses and still-flowering shrubs that made up the east garden that stood between them, and scented the air with their enticing fragrance. Wanted to tune out the sexy melody emanating from the radio playing softly from its perch on her bedside table. The same music she'd barely noticed only moments ago. The sun was setting, spreading pink and purple hues across the landscape, adding another layer of sensuality to her private fantasy as she imagined what it would be like to be in that room with him as she watched him move about.

When she could bear the tension no longer she jerked open the top drawer of the bureau and snagged her binoculars.

"You are truly pathetic," she muttered. She hadn't done anything this juvenile since she was seventeen. Even the knowledge that her current actions were more rash than her earlier display as a sex-starved nympho couldn't stop the compulsion now driving her. She had to see. She brought the binoculars her father had given her for bird watching on her twelfth birthday to her eyes and peered into Zach's bedroom window.

Suddenly she was a teenager again and her heart skittered in her chest. Her breath hitched when her gaze flowed over the wide planes of his shoulders, down his strong, bare back and to a lean waist. A towel hung loosely on his narrow hips. He was searching for something in his bureau. With every bend and reach, every twist, muscles flexed and contracted beneath tanned skin. He fished a pair of shorts from a drawer and grinned as if he'd hit pay dirt. That funny little flip-flop in her chest that always occurred whenever he smiled, did so even now with so much distance between them...with her peeping at him through ancient binoculars.

She'd seen Zach in swimming trunks dozens of times. She remembered what a great body he'd had, but it was even better now. Time and maturity had sculpted him a magnificent torso. Her respiration increased, keeping time with the impatient pounding in her chest. He dragged a T-shirt from another drawer and tossed it toward the bed to join the shorts he'd selected. Her gaze jerked back to that awesome chest where a sprinkling of silken hair adorned amazing pecs, then narrowed and plunged toward his naval. The outline of his lean hips was clear above the contrasting white towel.

"Mercy," she breathed. The man was gorgeous. The lightning quick combustion of heat deep inside her and the racing of her heart made it difficult to breathe. She had to stop this. She shouldn't be—

The towel dropped to the floor.

She gasped. Then stopped breathing altogether.

He moved toward the bed, his long legs all hard muscle...and, oh my dear, he was magnificent. He certainly hadn't been shorted in any department—not brains, not looks, not...she never imagined...

What was she doing?

Beth lowered the binoculars and spun away from the window. Belatedly, her mouth gaped. She'd been gawking at a stark naked Zach who had no idea he was being watched.

She was sick. Dragging in a ragged gulp of air, Beth shoved the damning binoculars back into the drawer and slammed it shut. Twenty-four hours in Zach's presence and already she'd regressed to those hormone-crazed, dreaded days when she'd thought of nothing else but him.

She had to get a grip. If he ever found out…

She shuddered. She didn't even want to think about that. After her little show this afternoon, he probably already thought she was a prime candidate for the psych ward. And maybe she was, because in spite of it all, she still wanted to go through with her decision to seduce him. The image of him standing there, completely, unabashedly naked, a semiarousal clearly delineating his well-endowed manhood formed in her head. Her pulse leapt as desire zinged through her. She wanted him all right. And, somehow, she intended to have him if just once. Then the mystery of him would be solved—mentally speaking. Lord knew she'd now seen all there was to see physically. They could be together…just once. Then she'd know he was just like any other man, admittedly an incredibly handsome and intelligent one who was seriously hung, a mere man nonetheless.

Her plan could prove once and for all that he wasn't the god she'd made him out to be all those years ago.

With that theory seen to fruition, maybe she could get over him *once and for all.*

Determined to plot a slightly more subtle but effective course, Beth headed out for a badly needed, stress-relieving run. She was going to do this her way, on her own terms. She grinned as she bounded through the kitchen door and down the steps. The charming, moderately arrogant Zach Ashton would be at her mercy.

Before he ever figured out what she was up to she would have proven her theory.

This time he would be the one left behind.

"FOR HEAVEN'S SAKE, you're not dressed," Colleen Ashton exclaimed, aghast, as Zach descended the staircase.

He glanced down at himself, then raised a skeptical eyebrow. "Of course, I am," he countered. "Just not for going out *out.*"

His mother waved a hand and huffed a breath. "I thought you might accompany us to dinner."

He stopped on the bottom tread and leaned against the polished mahogany newel post. "I don't think Harold would appreciate my presence," Zach teased. Harold Winthrop had courted his mother for seven years to no avail. Though Colleen enjoyed his attention and the perception of desirability cast for her peers to see, she had never once looked at any man seriously. Even after all these years she was still in love with Zach's father. He knew it and so did she. Now there was what a relationship was supposed to be, he reminded himself. And he had no clue how to make one like that happen. More proof that he wasn't worthy as husband material.

"You go right back up those stairs and get dressed," she ordered in her firmest don't-you-dare-argue-with-me tone. "Harold should simply consider himself lucky that I agree to have dinner with him at all."

Zach couldn't help a smile. "I'm quite sure he does."

Colleen assumed an expression of impatient tolerance. "Are you certain you won't join us, Zach. I hate to think of you here all alone."

He took the final step down, closed the distance

between them and deposited a heartfelt kiss on his mother's cheek. "Don't worry about me, I'm going for a run."

A frown furrowed her forehead. "You young people," she fussed. "You're always running from something."

If she only knew, Zach mused.

"I'll have dinner later. I'm sure I can rustle up something. You—" using one finger he tilted her chin upward and looked directly into her worried gray eyes "—have a good time." His smile widened to a grin. "And you tell Harold I'm quickly growing suspect of his intentions. Seven years is a long time."

She harrumphed. "This coming from a man who's yet to marry for the first time." She lifted one elegant eyebrow. "And who is rapidly nearing forty."

"I'm thirty-eight, so what?" Was everyone determined to remind him of his age? Zach crossed his arms over his chest and studied his mother with mounting suspicion. "If I didn't know you better I'd think you were teasing, but I know that look. Since when did you decide I need to get married?"

She daintily cleared her throat, a slight blush rising to her cheeks. "It is what most people do," she suggested from beneath lowered lashes. "I can't say that I don't have the occasional yearning for a grandchild."

The statement startled him, but he recovered swiftly. He rubbed his chin nonchalantly, somewhere in the back of his mind noting the five-o'clock shadow rasping against his palm. "A grandchild?" He considered that concept, carefully restraining the rush of emotions the sincere yearning in her eyes evoked. "I suppose I could work on that," he offered awkwardly. "But I can't promise you anything. You know I'm too busy for that kind of relationship."

She shook a manicured finger at him. "That attitude is a mistake Zacharius Ashton. You'll wake up one of these days and find yourself old and alone."

Zach held up both hands in surrender. "Okay, okay." He almost frowned at the vehemence in her tone. He'd never heard his mother speak so adamantly regarding the subject. Maybe it was the heart attack that had started her thinking of life's briefness. "I'll work on it," he promised with no idea how he would accomplish such a proposal.

She sighed, her shoulders sagged and she looked suddenly frail to him. "Helen had hoped Beth would…" she began, then seemed to realize what she was about to say and thought better of it.

He cocked his head. "What? That Beth would have a child? I suppose if that had happened the two of you might be on speaking terms now, for the child's sake," he suggested, the ire he instantly felt at the notion completely irrational.

Colleen squared her shoulders in defiance. "This has nothing to do with my relationship with Helen." She shrugged, an obvious attempt at appearing disinterested. "I just meant that Beth would probably remarry and produce a grandchild for Helen. I can only hope that you don't intend to leave me in the lurch."

The irritation he had no business feeling inched toward anger. "You're saying that Beth is involved?"

His mother looked taken aback, but not enough so to prevent her bloodhound instincts from kicking in.

"I'm not sure *involved* is the right word," she hedged.

"So she's dating," he countered, determined to have the meaning of her statement.

"Well, of course she is. She's a beautiful young woman. Smart, too. A doctor," she said with clear awe. "What man in his right mind wouldn't want her?"

Zach clenched his jaw. That shot had been aimed directly at him. He knew it. Was his mother on some sort of mission to throw him and Beth together? He stilled. Had she somehow talked Beth into some sort of crazy *grandchild* scheme? That would explain Beth's sudden about-face. At first she'd acted as if she didn't even want to be around him, then, the next thing he knew, she was kissing him.

"Mother, you haven't—" The doorbell sounded, cutting off his intended accusation.

"That's Harold. Have a pleasant run, Zach." She gifted him with a quick pat on the arm and hurried away in a rush of perfectly coifed gray hair and pink silk designer suit.

Zach shook his head and started for the back door. He had to be reading too much into his mother's comment. She would never attempt to interfere with his social life, not on that level anyway. And no way would Beth go along with such a ludicrous idea. The whole notion was outrageous. Apparently his little vacation was wreaking havoc with his ability to reason.

His mother indicated that Beth had a full social life. Did that mean that she was dating someone special right now? Then why had she kissed him like that today? He could still taste her lips. He licked his own. Could feel her body pressed against his. He'd wanted her in the worst way.

Enough, Ashton, he ordered, silently cursing himself for the fool he was. He wasn't supposed to be thinking about Beth or sex, he reminded himself. It took every ounce of determination he possessed to push aside that line of thinking, but he managed.

ZACH JOGGED at a steady pace for about twenty minutes, his focus trained on work and what he might be missing. He'd given Victoria a call that morning and she had assured him that all was well. But still, he missed being there. He missed the exhilarating adrenaline rush of a major legal coup. He missed it all—getting up at the crack of dawn to run, reviewing cases with Victoria and Ian, working until seven or eight and having dinner and an occasional evening of physical pleasure with a lady friend. What else could a man ask for?

Beth's deep brown eyes zoomed into vivid focus, fracturing all other thought. Everything about her— the sound of her voice, her sweet smell, the feel of her skin—tumbled into his head, wrecking any hope of keeping thoughts of her away. How would he ever survive the next two weeks? As much as he loved his mother, coming back home was proving one huge mistake.

There were far too many memories here. Instantly, Beth's taste sprang to mind. He clenched his jaw and tried to ignore the hunger gnawing at him. How was it he could still want her so badly? She was beautiful and he had loved her for as long as he could remember, but that love was supposed to be the brother-sister kind now. After all, she'd married someone else. He should have moved on...thought he had.

He called himself every kind of idiot as he lunged forward, increasing his pace, trying to outrun his thoughts. His mother's words, *you're always running from something,* echoed in his ears. Was she that perceptive, or was he simply that easy to read? He was running, all right. Running from what Beth made him feel...from the past he couldn't change.

And now his mother laid another guilt trip on him, a grandchild. How was he supposed to accomplish that monumental task? Well, he knew how to do it. That wasn't the problem. Marriage usually came before kids, and Zach had no intention of getting married at this stage in his life. Therein lay the point at issue. He liked his life just as it was. He'd made the decision long ago, and it was too late to change his mind now. Though he loved women, and definitely enjoyed his share, there was no one he wanted to spend his life with.

Well...no one that he could have anyway.

It was just too late.

The sound of footfalls echoing his own registered in his awareness about three seconds before he collided with a warm, decidedly feminine, body.

Their arms and legs tangled. He instinctively rolled to catch the brunt of the fall as they plunged toward the ground. His left shoulder hit the ground first, her slight weight slamming into his midsection as he flattened firmly against the grass. The added force sent the air rushing out of his lungs on an audible grunt.

"Are you all right?"

It was Beth. She was suddenly hovering over him.

The last of the setting sun's light silhouetting her profile, giving her image a surreal quality. Zach blinked, uncertain as to whether she was real or if he'd somehow conjured her up. He shook his head and started to sit up. A sharp jab of pain in his shoulder startled a groan from him.

"Don't move."

"I'm okay," he snapped, irritated with himself for not paying better attention. He pushed to a sitting position, ignoring his body's protest.

"Let me have a look," she said, her voice still soft, but her tone firmer.

He swept the hair back from his face with his right hand and nodded in acquiescence. Why the hell not complete his humiliation? The feel of her warm, soft fingers on his skin as she carefully dragged his T-shirt up and then off almost toppled his already unsteady composure and chased away all other thought. She leaned closer, the brush of her breasts teasing his skin.

He was in trouble.

"Does this hurt?" She gently probed his back a few inches below his shoulder.

"No," he replied, the word clipped with the tension rocketing through him.

Her fingers moved higher. He winced, then snapped again, "I'm fine, really."

"Of course you are." She probed deeper. He clenched his jaw to prevent another groan from escaping. "Just bruised, I think." She finally offered his T-shirt back.

"So, I'll live?" He started to tug his shirt on but reconsidered when the move sent another searing throb through his shoulder.

"You'll live."

He stood and held out his right hand to assist her. "You're not hurt?"

She peered up at him, searching his eyes far too closely. "Nope. You saw to that."

He shrugged his good shoulder. "I guess I was distracted. I didn't see you coming. Taking the brunt of the fall was the least I could do."

"I didn't see you either." She grinned sheepishly. "Maybe we need a yield sign at the intersection of these two paths."

Damn, she looked good. The running shorts displayed those shapely thighs...making his mouth go suddenly dry. The cropped tank top showcased more than it concealed. The silky skin of her midriff made him yearn to touch her. But it was the way the material clung to her breasts that did him in. He didn't want to stare, but he just couldn't help himself.

"You're sure you're okay?" she asked, drawing his attention to her pretty face. "You look a little shaken."

Shaken? Oh yeah, he was definitely shaken. Long wisps of honey-colored hair had worked loose from her ponytail and now clung to her slender throat. She licked those lush lips and something lurched inside him. It was all he could do not to reach out for her.

"Well," she said when he failed to respond, "I'll try to watch where I'm going in the future."

"Me, too," he mumbled. His gaze connected with hers and need seared straight through him, leaving him weak with want.

She stepped nearer, worry marring her features as she studied him more closely. "Maybe I'll just walk back to the house with you."

"I'm fine, really," he repeated.

Something distinctly sexual glittered in those deep chocolate-brown depths. "Why don't you let me be the judge of that?" she suggested in a voice husky with what sounded like desire. She slid her arm around his waist. "Just lean on me and I'll take good care of you." She smiled up at him. "After all, I am a doctor. I probably know more about you than you know about yourself."

He was definitely in trouble.

Chapter Five

Beth surveyed the living room of the cottage to make sure her mother was not in the room, then promptly slammed the front door behind her and stamped her foot with the fury she could no longer contain. Never in her entire life had she been so angry. Zach had blown her off yet again.

Halfway to his house he'd insisted that he was fine and could make it the rest of the way without any help. She had known perfectly well he didn't need her help. She'd planned on laying on a little more temptation, then maybe…

And he'd dismissed her as if she were twelve and too young to be alone in the house with him. Thursday was Mrs. Ashton's night out with Mr. Winthrop. Beth had all but done a little victory dance at the good fortune of the timing. She could play doctor examining his shoulder again, one thing would likely lead to another and they'd wind up in his room…in his bed. Beth swallowed tightly at the images summoned by that thought. The memory of watching his every move through the binoculars, the towel dropping, the perfection of his male body joined her kaleidoscope of memories. In spite of her fury, her body responded instantly. Her pulse tripped, her heart pounded, her skin heated.

She sighed a defeated sound as she threaded her fingers through her disheveled hair, loosening it the rest of the way from its confines. Why did he always push her away? What was it about her that made him back off each time they got close? She wasn't his sister. They weren't related at all. And she was well past the age of consent. Why couldn't he just let it happen? She was a woman, he was a man, end of subject.

Tossing aside the clip that had held her hair she trudged off in the direction of the kitchen. Maybe dinner and quality time with her mom would take her mind off Zach and his infuriating hang-up where she was concerned. Beth hoped that her mother and Mrs. Ashton had made amends by now. On the rare occasions when there was a dispute, the two had never stayed angry with each other for more than a few hours. Considering their ages and Mrs. Ashton's recent health problems now was not the time to start. Not to mention it would take the birthday party worries off Beth's back. She didn't even want to think about that. But she would have to, and very soon.

Exiling thoughts of Zach and Mrs. Ashton for the time being, she focused on finding her mother. The empty kitchen drew the corners of Beth's mouth downward. Helen hadn't said anything about going out. Her car was outside. A sniffling sound drew Beth's attention toward the laundry room door. Her sneakers silent on the stone floor she made her way across the room, then hesitated in the partially open doorway. Her mother was sorting laundry—Beth's laundry.

"Mom, I was going to do that," she protested.

Helen spun around, clearly startled. She blinked, then smiled, quickly swiping her damp cheeks. "Oh, I didn't realize you were home."

Beth grabbed a wad of colored clothing and started to layer it into the washing machine. She struggled to remain calm when she wanted desperately to demand an explanation of why her mother was crying, but that tactic would get her nowhere.

"I don't mind doing your laundry," Helen offered, her tone too chipper. "Your father and I waited a very long time to have you, and now you're all grown up. Doing little things like this for you makes me feel needed."

"Mom!" Her words squeezed Beth's heart. She grabbed her mother's arm and forced her to stop sorting and look directly at her. "Of course you're needed. Why would you say such a thing?"

"Don't overreact, dear," Helen scolded affectionately. "I didn't mean it the way it sounded. I just meant that I enjoy doing things for you."

Beth wasn't convinced. She braced her hands on her hips and searched her mother's eyes, which were still a little red and suspiciously bright. "You're not acting like yourself," she accused gently. "Does this have anything to do with the falling out between you and Colleen?"

Helen trained her attention back on the mounds of sorted clothing. "I told you I didn't want to talk about that."

Exasperated, Beth placed one hand over her mother's, stilling her movements. "I wish you'd confide in me. I can't bear seeing you like this and not being able to do anything."

Helen settled a somber gaze on hers. "You shouldn't dwell on it. There's nothing you can do. Unless Colleen has a change of heart, there's nothing anyone can do." She drew in a deep, shuddering breath. "I'll simply have to live with it."

"This doesn't make sense," Beth argued. "Why would you have to live with whatever it is? It's a free country, Mother, you can do whatever you feel is right."

"I made a promise that I can't break."

"Can't or won't?"

Her mother leaned against the dryer as if she suddenly felt too tired to support her own weight. "Does it matter? There are some things that are bigger than you are and you can only pray that the decision you make is the right one."

Beth suppressed the urge to shake her head. "What could possibly be that big?"

Helen turned back to the chore at hand. "I think after I finish this laundry I'll make a nice salad for our dinner. With shredded ham and all your other favorites."

Beth admitted defeat. She wasn't going to get her mother to confide in her, that was crystal clear. But she had to find a way to get the two older women to reach some sort of understanding and make amends. Things just couldn't go on this way. But Beth couldn't do this alone, she would need help.

Zach's help.

She would simply have to set her seduction plan aside until they figured out this thing between their mothers. Beth had waited this long to have him, a few more days wouldn't hurt her.

ZACH WASHED his second sandwich down with a tall glass of cold milk. He wiped his mouth and set the glass on the counter. He felt better already. His shoulder still hurt like hell, but at least he could think straight again. It was amazing how much better a guy could think on a full stomach. Smoothing a hand over his abdomen he admitted the truth of the matter. His temporary loss of equilibrium had nothing to do with food or the lack thereof. Beth had knocked him off his feet, literally and figuratively. He'd been dazed for a few minutes there, unable to focus on anything but her nearness. Not even the slickest legal opponent he'd faced in his career had ever shaken him like that, and certainly no other woman had confused him so.

Luckily he'd regained his senses before they were inside the house together…alone. That would surely have proven disastrous. He knew it as well as he knew his own name. Whatever was going on in Beth's pretty little head he wasn't going to be a party to it…if he could help it. Many more let's-get-physical episodes like this latest one and he might not be able to control himself. Right now he needed a hot shower to soothe his bruised muscles. All he had to do was figure out a way to block thoughts of Beth.

Yeah, right.

She was like an intriguing case, he couldn't keep his mind off her.

A loud rap at the kitchen door stalled him halfway across the room. Surely Beth hadn't come to check up on him. He wasn't ready for another tension-filled confrontation with her. And he damned sure wasn't ready to play doctor. But his mother wouldn't be back for a couple more hours, who else could it be?

Resigned to the inevitable, Zach made his way to the door. He hesitated for a moment, considering that he still wore the running shorts…and nothing else. He hadn't showered since he'd opted to eat first. He definitely needed a shave. His appearance had gone to hell since arriving, but then, that was the point of a vacation, wasn't it? Kick back, no suits and ties. Besides, he was trying to ward Beth off not lure her in.

Satisfied with his rationale he opened the door. His gaze connected with her worried brown eyes then instinctively slid down her body. She was still wearing her running attire as well. The barely-there tank top still molded to her breasts…the shorts showed off those gorgeous legs just the way he remembered. His gaze traveled back up the length of her. But now her hair was down, hanging around her slender shoulders like silky wisps of spun gold. He tried to swallow but couldn't manage the task.

"We have to talk," she deadpanned.

"You're right," he said huskily. "We do need to…talk." He opened the door wider and stepped aside, inviting her into the house. The *empty* house. His next breath fell short of reaching his lungs. *Get ahold of yourself, man,* he ordered. This is Beth. She's practically your sister. And she picked another man to be her husband. She didn't wait for you. A prick of ire needled him with that last thought.

He closed the door and faced her. She was inspecting him as thoroughly as he had her only seconds before. His body tensed beneath her deliberate survey, each muscle hardening. His good intentions were going south fast.

"You said we needed to talk." He leaned against the nearest counter and crossed his arms over his chest since her visual examination seemed to have stalled there.

Her gaze snapped up to his and she blinked. "I found my mother crying a few minutes ago," she told him, her tone a little unsteady.

A new kind of tension trickled through him. "Is she ill?" The image of the woman who'd been like a second mother to him flashed through his mind. Helen McCormick was family. Beth was family. Somehow he had to get all this other *stuff* into perspective. If there was anything Helen needed he would move heaven and earth to see that she got it.

Beth shook her head. "Physically she's fine. It's her emotional well-being I'm concerned about." She folded her arms over her breasts. The breasts he wanted so to touch. Zach cursed himself silently. He would not treat Beth like a sex object. She wasn't like the women he dated in Chicago...she was...

Dammit, he was supposed to be concentrating on Helen's situation. "What happened?" He wanted to reach out to Beth, to offer her a comforting hand, but he was afraid if he touched her he'd do something truly stupid. "Tell me exactly what happened," he urged.

"It's this standoff between our mothers." She stared directly at him, her eyes relaying the depth of her worry. "I don't know what's going on between them, but it's not a simple misunderstanding. This is big, Zach. Big enough to destroy what they've had together for more than forty years."

He frowned at that idea. He couldn't imagine his mother turning her back on her oldest and dearest friend. Surely the tiff would blow over. "Did Helen say that?"

"That's just it. She won't say anything other than she made a promise and she can't break it. She did tell me that there was something that needed to be said, but that only your mother could do the saying."

Zach tried to reassure her with his eyes since touching her wasn't a good idea. "I'll talk to my mother and get this straightened out. I'm sure I can make her see reason."

Beth sighed. "I don't think it's going to be that easy. I'm afraid it's going to take some major interference on our part to resolve whatever this is."

A grin tickled his lips. Unable to hold it back, the gesture spread across his face. "Are you suggesting that we manipulate our mothers?"

She lifted her chin a notch in defiance of his censuring tone, jest or not. "I'm suggesting that we do whatever it takes. Considering your mother's heart attack, and both their ages, I say we'd be foolish not to intervene."

There was no denying those two facts. "Agreed," he allowed with a hint of reservation. He didn't like the idea of interfering in his mother's life any more than he would appreciate her meddling in his.

"You don't sound so sure."

He inclined his head and studied her more closely. "Let's just say I like to keep my options open. But I do agree that we should do something."

She nodded once. "Good. That's settled then. We'll each give it some thought and then we'll discuss it further tomorrow."

"Fine." When she lingered, her gaze once more tracing his frame, he added, "Was there something else you wanted to say?"

Those dark, chocolate-colored eyes were frank and determined when they met his again. She wanted to do more than talk. He tensed, resisting the urge to grab her and drag her upstairs before she could say a word.

"Just one more thing." She moved a step closer, sending his tension to a new level. "I've tried to make it clear, but subtlety isn't going to work with you. So, I'll just say it so there's no misunderstanding…. I want to have an affair with you."

Stunned didn't begin to describe the impact her statement had. "You want to what?" he said hoarsely.

Zach looked as startled as Beth felt. Had she really said that? Dear God, she had. It was too late to take it back now. She squared her shoulders and stared at his handsome face, avoiding eye contact. "I said, I want to have an affair with you. Do you have a problem with that?"

A kind of shock captured his features. "I need a drink." He bolted for the door.

Her fury igniting all over again, Beth followed him to the parlor. He rounded the bar and prowled through the bottles until he found what he was looking for.

He poured a healthy serving of whiskey into a glass and offered it to her, but didn't make eye contact. She declined with a shake of her head, which he must have noted in his peripheral vision because he sure wouldn't look directly at her. He downed the liquor in one swallow and set the glass aside with a heavy *thwack*.

Those blue eyes settled on hers then and Beth knew she'd just been introduced to the legendary attorney, Zacharius Ashton. That steely gaze gave away nothing of what he might be thinking. Not even a hint of emotion showed itself.

He braced his hands wide apart on the bar's polished black granite surface and leaned forward just enough to lend intimidation to his stance. ''You want to have sex with me, is that it?''

His crude words almost sent her scrambling for the door, but she held her ground. She fixed her hands firmly on her hips and met his hard, analyzing gaze. ''That's right.'' She lifted one shoulder in a half shrug. ''I'm attracted to you, you're attracted to me, why not? People do it all the time.''

A muscle in his chiseled jaw jumped. Beth chewed her lower lip to prevent a tiny smile. Now she was getting somewhere. That legal eagle armor wasn't nearly as impervious as she'd first thought. She could crack it. All she had to do was be persistent.

''We're practically family,'' he challenged, inflection still lacking in his tone.

''No, we're not. Besides, I know what I felt when we kissed this afternoon. You're just as interested as I am.'' She had him there. Let him try and deny that.

Something glimmered in his eyes…uncertainty, maybe. ''You caught me off guard. It was a typical male reflex.''

She did smile then. ''Look me straight in the eye, Zach Ashton, and tell me that you're not attracted to me.'' She edged another step closer, leaving nothing but the narrow span of granite separating them. "Tell me you don't want me."

That muscle flexed in his jaw again. "I won't lie to you, Beth. You're a beautiful woman. Of course, I'm attracted to you. But you're not my type."

She didn't miss the flicker of relief in those baby blues with that statement. He'd just chalked one up to the defense.

"Is that right?"

"That's right." His gaze never left hers. "I don't do affairs. I do *sex*. If you're looking for anything other than that, then you're looking in the wrong place. I'm not the marrying kind."

Touché. So he thought she was looking for another husband. "Don't flatter yourself. I'm not looking for a proposal. You think I'm not capable of a one-night stand? I was married, Zach, and I've had other relationships," she fibbed, exaggerating her few dates before marrying Matt. "And whether you want to admit it or not, I am all grown up. I'm a woman, I have needs. You're here, I'm here, what's the big deal?"

Anger, swift and unmistakable, kindled in his eyes. "So, I'm convenient, is that it?" He poured another drink and downed it as quickly as the first. "Fine. Why don't we just do it now and get it over with? I can be ready any time."

Beth jerked back a step, her eyes wide with astonishment. Who was backpedaling now? Zach mused. A smile kicked up one corner of his mouth. He'd had a feeling all that sass was just a bluff.

"I wasn't suggesting that we…" She struggled with her words. "…start at this exact moment. I mean…" Color rose up her neck and spread across her cheeks. "We should choose a time and place to...well, to..."

He cocked one eyebrow and eyed her skeptically. "You mean, make an *appointment*."

She took yet another step backward. "Not precisely an appointment." She flared her palms upward. "More like a date."

"Do you usually set dates to have sex?" he asked pointedly. When faced with her look of horror he instantly regretted the remark. He didn't want to have this conversation...not with Beth.

"We..." She visibly grappled for an explanation. "We really have to straighten out this mess between our mothers before we think of ourselves," she said in a rush. Relief immediately flowed over her pretty face.

He couldn't argue that. "You're right. We'll decide what we're going to do about those two and then we'll have sex."

She nodded stiffly. "Sounds good." More space appeared between them as she moved farther away. "I'll call you tomorrow."

Zach watched that amazing derriere sway subtly as she walked toward the door. Taking a deep breath was impossible with those long legs and that shapely backside drawing the attention of his every brain cell.

"Beth," he called out to her before she could get completely away.

She paused at the door and looked back at him. "Yes."

She appeared much more relaxed with this much distance between them. She looked so young...so innocent. How the hell was he going to save her from him—much less herself?

"If you change your mind," he began, knowing it was the only right thing to do, "I'll understand."

She smiled, the gesture clearly forced. "Why would I change my mind?"

For two long beats he just looked at her, taking in the whole picture: silky, honey-colored hair, wide doe eyes and a face straight out of heaven. An angel. Sweet, Beth. Dr. Elizabeth McCormick, who spent her days healing the sick and her nights sharing her childhood home with her mother.

And he was the devil himself. He'd never once in his adult life done even one thing so selfless as what she did on a daily basis. He didn't deserve her. She'd obviously known that when she picked another man over him. He gritted his teeth. There was no point in denying it now. "Because you're a good girl and I'm not sure you really want what you've asked for."

She only looked at him for one long moment, then said, "I'm not that little girl next door you used to know, Zach." She smiled, a seriously wicked gesture. "You'll see."

She was gone before he could say another word. He blew out a breath and scrubbed a hand over his face. Though physically he was more than ready to charge full-steam ahead, on a mental level he knew that he had to tread very carefully here. It would be so easy to take what she offered, but that would be a mistake. Any kind of permanent relationship between them would be geographically impossible…not to mention the dedication to duty required by his post at the Colby Agency. She was as dedicated to hers as he was to his. Neither would want to change.

Besides, Beth was still young. She would eventually want to marry again and have children. Zach wasn't at all sure if he could give himself to her so completely and then watch her marry someone else. The first time had been hard enough. The memory of seeing her with *him* still burned in his gut.

At least now he knew what she was up to...what she wanted from him. Sex. She probably saw him as some sort of conquest—the older guy who'd ignored her as a kid. Anger swelled inside him at the thought that he might not mean any more to her than that.

An epiphany struck and a wide smile slid across his face. Well, if his undivided attention was what she wanted, he would give it to her in a form befitting his infamous reputation back in Chicago. If little Beth McCormick thought she was woman enough for him, she should just bring it on.

But Zach had a feeling that it would never happen. All he had to do was pour on the charm and the sexual advances and she would run like a scared rabbit.

He groaned when he considered that it was going to take another cold shower to get his body back under control.

Maybe saving Beth from herself could be his one totally selfless act.

BY LUNCHTIME the next day Beth had resigned herself to the fact that she was going to have to take drastic measures to prove to Zach that she wasn't the *good little girl* he thought she was. Well, at least not that good anyway. She could be wicked when the urge struck her.

"Hey, Beth, how about lunch?"

She glanced up from the pile of reports on her desk

to find Lucy, her friend and a staff nurse, lounging against her doorjamb. Beth produced a belated smile. "Thanks, but I have some errands to run."

"Another day then. We need to catch up. It seems like forever since we've really talked."

"Next week for sure." Beth dug for her appointment calendar. "I'm penciling you in right now."

Lucy gave her a thumbs-up. "Sounds good."

After her friend had gone, Beth glanced at the telephone and considered calling her mother again. But she'd already checked on her once today. If she called a second time, Helen would only be suspicious.

Beth snagged up her purse and headed for the door. She'd hardly slept at all last night. Every word Zach had said to her, the images of his naked, muscled body had swirled in her head all night long. She was scared to death that he was actually going to take her up on her offer, and at the same time frightened that his conscience would regain control and he'd deny her.

She would never be able to get on with her life if she didn't get him out of her system once and for all. She'd come this far, there was no use backing out now.

Fifteen minutes later, Beth stood in front of a local Cartersville shop. One that neither she nor anyone she even knew had ever been inside. The sign above the door read We Tattoo You. She dragged in a deep, bolstering breath and shoved the door inward before she could lose her nerve.

A bell jingled and a half-dozen or so suspicious gazes focused on her. Beth swallowed, her throat almost too dry to perform the function.

One particularly large—huge actually—guy stepped forward. He wore the kind of biker attire one saw in the movies. He looked grungy and meaner than any character she'd ever seen on the big screen.

She straightened her light wool suit jacket and managed to ask, "Are you the owner?"

"Lady," he growled, taking yet another step in her direction, "you can go right back to that health department and tell those communist inspectors I said to go to—"

"I'm—" Beth retreated a few inches. "I'm not from the health department," she assured him quickly.

He relaxed visibly. "Are you lost?"

She shook her head. "No…"

Renewed suspicion narrowed his gaze. "Then what the hell are you doing here?"

She moistened her lips and gathered her crumbling composure. "I need to change my image." She looked the big guy right in the eye. "Can you help me with that?"

A dentally challenged grin broke across his face. "Lady, you've come to the right place."

BETH HAD JUST ten minutes before she had to be back at the hospital, but there was still time to pay for her items. She quickly scanned the array of sexy, silk lingerie she had selected. She resisted the urge to lift her blouse and look at her belly button. She still couldn't believe she'd actually done it. She would absolutely have died if anyone she knew had walked into that tattoo parlor and found her there. Big Bart, the owner, had personally performed the little change she'd finally decided upon. She blushed at the memory of the audience who'd watched the entire procedure.

Well, she'd wanted a change.

She raised a skeptical eyebrow as she surveyed the thong panties she'd picked out. She'd never worn anything so...so racy.

She had to do it. She had to prove to Zach that she wasn't that naive young woman he used to know. She was an adult. She had every intention of making him wish he'd noticed a whole lot sooner.

The musical notes emanating from her purse drew her attention there. She fished her cell phone out and flipped open the mouthpiece and offered a brisk hello.

"Beth?"

It was Zach. Beth's eyes widened and she dropped the thong she'd been holding.

"Yes," she croaked. A blush heated her cheeks.

"I thought I'd check to see if you were ready to discuss the situation with our mothers."

Relief flooded her. She'd been afraid he'd ask if she was ready to—

"Have you come up with anything yet?" he prodded when she hesitated.

"I have a patient waiting for me right now," she lied. "Meet me tonight and we'll come up with something."

She held her breath until he answered.

"Where?" The one word was husky, filled with sensual innuendo.

"At the swing," she said quickly. "After dinner. See you then." Beth depressed the end button before he could say anything else. Her heart was pounding.

Her palms were perspiring. Her knees felt weak. All from simply hearing his voice.

What would she do tonight when they were alone with nothing but the moonlight as chaperone?

Chapter Six

Zach waited patiently by the big oak. He'd had dinner with his mother already. Every attempt he'd made to bring up Helen had quickly been diverted to some other subject. Colleen Ashton was quite adept at avoiding what she had no desire to discuss. Knowing when he was outmaneuvered, Zach relented to her choice of conversation topics—her birthday. He wondered if Beth had come up with a theme yet. A smile nudged at the corners of his mouth. Poor Beth. She'd really gotten the short end of that stick. But she hadn't complained, not really.

Darkness had fallen quickly after he came outside. He leaned against the oak's trunk and wondered what was keeping Beth. He studied the stone cottage across the garden, the moonlight making it look every bit as magical as he always deemed it to be. But the princess who lived there was still a no-show. He couldn't be that early. Maybe she was making him wait. Women loved to play games.

But this wasn't just any woman…this was Beth.

Restless, he set the swing into motion and watched its hypnotic sway. Mr. McCormick had crafted the seat by hand, smoothing the wood until it was as slick as glass. Then he'd climbed the oak to hang the sturdy ropes. Though it had been more than twenty years since he'd first hung the swing, Zach remembered the event as if it had happened just yesterday. He'd helped by telling Mr. McCormick when the seat hung evenly. Then Zach had spent countless hours pushing Beth in the thing. She'd squealed with delight and begged him to push her higher.

She'd owned his heart even then.

That was a very long time ago, he reminded himself, annoyed with his uncharacteristic sentimentality. He and Beth had different lives now, were different people. If she'd had any interest in marrying him, she wouldn't have married someone else. It was true that as a kid she'd idolized him, but when she grew up she'd chosen someone else to share her life. Her divorce had only been final a month or so according to his mother. His brow furrowed as he analyzed that aspect of Beth's current behavior. Maybe her focus on him was nothing more than a rebound reaction. She might feel compelled to prove she was still desirable.

If only she knew.

Quite possibly she considered Zach safe. He stilled, turning that concept over in his mind. She could enjoy a fun romp, then not have to worry about facing him on a regular basis when it was over because he'd be back in Chicago. Only human, he'd like nothing better than to participate, but it would be a mistake. It would forever change their lifelong relationship. Things would never be the same again. As much as he wanted her and hated the fact that she'd once belonged to someone else, he wouldn't risk what they had for a brief affair.

And it would be just an affair. Her life was here, his was back at the agency. He couldn't stay, she wouldn't want to go. It was the proverbial lose-lose situation. Somehow he had to make her see that this whole idea was a mistake.

The best course, as he saw it, was to put a little reverse psychology into play. He knew Beth too well. She was the quintessential good girl. All he had to do was play his part right and she'd run like hell.

The sound of a door closing drew his attention to the cottage. Beth walked slowly in his direction. His body reacted instantly to the simple act of looking at her.

The breeze kicked up, lifting her golden tresses and swirling them around her shoulders. She'd changed clothes, he realized as his gaze swept down her body. He knew she'd worn green slacks and a blazer to work that morning because he'd watched her go. He had a great view of the east garden and the cottage from his bedroom window. As she neared now, he noted the way a pale blue blouse molded to her slender torso, defining each firm breast. Matching slacks, that fit more like a second skin, outlined her shapely legs.

"I hope I didn't keep you waiting." She sat down on the smooth wooden seat of the swing as if it were twenty years ago and she fully expected him to give her a push.

Zach crossed his legs at the ankles and folded his arms over his chest. "No problem. I've been refining my plan." Which was true, she didn't need to know which plan he meant.

She looked up at him, the moonlight spilling over her, giving her an ethereal glow. Just what he needed, another reminder that she wasn't the kind of woman a man took to bed and walked away from. No wonder she'd picked another guy to marry, she was definitely too sweet for Zach. He liked his women sex hot and wild. Beth deserved better than what he had to offer her. Two weeks wasn't nearly enough for a good affair.

"You have a plan? Good." She pushed the swing into a slow glide with one foot. "What do I need to do?"

Zach decided that looking directly at her and allowing her to see how she affected him physically was the right way to go. "I'll ask my mother to meet me at Pearle's for lunch tomorrow. You do the same with Helen."

Beth didn't seem put off by his steady gaze, instead, she pursed her lush lips and considered his proposal for a moment, then asked, "What's to keep them from walking out when they see each other instead of us?"

Zach grinned. "That's the beauty of it. There's no way my mother would ever make a public spectacle in Pearle's. She'll sit through lunch if it kills her."

A tiny smile played about the corners of Beth's mouth. "You're right. That could work." She stood, apparently assuming that their decision was the end of the discussion. "What time should we tell them to meet us?"

"Noon. That's the busiest time. I'll make the arrangements with the maitre d'."

"I hope your plan works. We can't let whatever this is keep stewing between them."

He straightened from his relaxed stance. "Agreed." Time to put his *other* plan into high gear.

"Have you decided when *we're* going to get to-gether?"

She faltered visibly at the question. "I...today was really busy. I didn't have a chance to give it much thought."

Zach closed the distance between them with slow, deliberate steps. That deer-caught-in-the-headlights look widened her eyes. "I haven't thought about much else," he returned softly. He trailed a finger down her arm. She shivered. Desire struck him hard and low as his fingers closed around hers. "Patience is not one of my strong points."

"It should be soon," she said quickly. "I just have to check my schedule."

He angled his head and searched her eyes as best he could in the moonlight. "You haven't changed your mind, have you?"

All signs of doubt disappeared instantly. "Of course not." Taking a deep breath, for courage, he supposed, she tiptoed and pressed a chaste kiss to his lips. "I can't wait," she murmured.

His free arm went around her waist and he pulled her firmly against him, making sure her softness molded fully to the proof of his own anticipation. "Why wait?" He closed his mouth over hers before she could respond.

To his surprise, she didn't resist him. Instead, she draped her arms around his neck and leaned into the kiss. She drank greedily of all he had to offer, her mouth tempting his in every way. So hot, so sweet...and so very needy. He could feel her des-peration as she practically writhed in his arms. Her neediness sent his senses spiraling out of control. He wanted to do whatever it took to make her happy...to satisfy her. He wanted to make love to her as no one else ever had. He cradled her head and deepened the kiss, thrusting his tongue inside her mouth. She whimpered softly and glided her hot tongue along the length of his. Desire erupted inside him.

He had to have her.

His hands slid down her back and over her heart-shaped bottom. He lifted her against him and stumbled toward the oak. Leaning her against the trunk, he pulled her legs up around his waist so that he could grind the ache in his loins into her feminine heat. She arched into him. He groaned. She made a tiny sound, almost a cry. Her fingers plowed into his hair, crushing his mouth more fully into hers. The hard, jutting peaks of her breasts seared his chest. He cupped her bottom, his fingers squeezing the tightly encased flesh.

He had to get her in the house...to his car... somewhere so they would have some privacy. The gazebo flashed through his mind followed by the vivid image of making love to Beth on that wooden floor. Reason intruded like a blast of icy water.

What was he doing?

He couldn't take Beth like this. He stopped. Hadn't he already decided that taking her at all would be a mistake? He drew his mouth from hers. Her ragged breath sizzled over his sensitized lips.

She stiffened in his arms, reason apparently overtaking her once more as well. "Oh, God." She scrambled away from him before he could stop her. "I have to go." She shoved a handful of hair behind her ear and hugged her arms around her middle in a protective manner. "I'll see you at noon tomorrow."

All he could manage was a curt nod. His entire

body was hot and throbbing, aching for her. But all he could do was watch her go. When he'd recovered his composure, he turned and started toward the house.

Well, he thought dryly, so much for reverse psychology.

COLLEEN ENTERED Pearle's, her absolute favorite restaurant in Cartersville, one minute past the hour. She hated to be late, even one minute, but there was nothing for it. Bernard, the maitre d', gifted her with a wide smile and offered his arm.

"Good afternoon, Mrs. Ashton. It's a pleasure to see you today. I hope you're doing well."

"It's good to be alive, Bernie," she said in all honesty. "I'm doing quite well, thank you."

"When Mr. Ashton called, I made sure your favorite table on the mezzanine was reserved."

Colleen patted his arm. "You know how I love that view of the atrium."

"Yes, ma'am."

Bernie escorted her up the short flight of stairs and to the same small table for two she'd asked for since the restaurant opened almost thirty years ago. It was her table and everyone from the maitre d's to the busboys knew it.

"Enjoy your lunch." Bernie pulled back her chair and rushed away before she could even sit down.

Frowning at his sudden loss of decorum, Colleen took her seat. "I wonder what put a burr under his saddle." She glanced across the table to admonish Zach for not acknowledging her arrival just as the large menu blocking him from view lowered.

Helen sat in the opposite chair.

"You!" Helen gasped. "What are *you* doing here?"

"I beg your pardon," Colleen replied in a stage whisper, glancing first left, then right to make sure no one had heard the outburst. "This is *my* table."

Fury streaked across Helen's face. "I don't see your name on it, you pompous—"

"Don't you dare make a scene," Colleen cut her off, in the calmest voice she could muster. "My son asked me to have lunch with him here. This is *my* table."

"Beth asked me to meet her here for lunch," Helen countered. "And this is the table I was shown to."

Colleen's gaze narrowed. So, this was the way of it. "I smell a rat," she muttered more to herself than to her reluctant luncheon companion.

Realization appeared to dawn on Helen at that moment as well. "They wouldn't," she said in disbelief.

"Excuse me, Mrs. Ashton," a waiter interrupted. "Mr. Ashton asked me to give you this."

Colleen accepted the envelope and thanked the waiter. She looked first at Helen, then at her own name scrawled across the pristine white envelope in Zach's bold handwriting. She couldn't believe her own son would set her up this way.

"Read it," Helen urged, clearly impatient to be on her way.

Ignoring the sting to her feelings that accompanied her friend's tone, Colleen opened the envelope and quickly read the short note, her suspicions confirmed.

"Out loud," Helen snapped.

Colleen made a resigned sound and obeyed.

"Mother, this is for your own good. Make up with Helen. We'll be watching. Love, Zach."

Silence reigned supreme for three long beats. Colleen refolded the note and laid it aside. This had gone too far. Why couldn't Helen see that she was wrong? Why couldn't things go back to the way they used to be?

"This mess we've made is beginning to affect them," Helen said tightly. "We can't go on this way."

Colleen's gaze snapped to hers. "Did you think they wouldn't notice? You must admit that you've been rather open with the whole mess."

Helen's lips tightened into a thin line.

Colleen sighed wearily. "I'm too old for this. If our friendship has ever meant anything to you, why can't you just leave it alone?"

Helen started to rise from her chair. "We have nothing to talk about."

Heads would be turning their way any second. Colleen snagged her by the arm. "Don't you dare walk out on me here. Sit down and have lunch. It's on me."

"I don't want lunch," Helen said crisply.

"We have to talk about the children," Colleen offered quickly, in hopes of defusing the situation.

Wariness slipping into her expression, Helen resumed her seat. "What about the children?"

Relief sped through Colleen's veins. While she didn't want Helen to make a scene in Pearle's, of all places, more than that, Colleen didn't want this standoff to continue. She wanted Helen to see things her way.

"Are you ladies ready?" The waiter paused at their table once more.

"Let's order," Colleen suggested, "and then we'll talk."

After their selections were placed, Helen's grudgingly, the waiter scurried away with a promise to bring their drinks.

"I'm waiting," Helen insisted.

"They must have plotted this little tactic last night," Colleen began, glancing around. "According to Zach's note, they're in here somewhere watching us."

"What makes you think they planned this last night?" Helen countered. "Other than a short walk, Beth was at home all evening."

"I saw them," Colleen told her, a knowing quality in her voice. She also knew what she'd seen.

Helen's brow creased. "Where?"

"Out by the swing."

"How do you know they were talking about us?"

Colleen exhaled her impatience. "Because my son asked me to lunch immediately after he came inside."

"That—" Helen snapped her mouth shut while the waiter deposited their drinks before them. As soon as he'd ensured they required nothing else of him at the moment he walked away. Helen continued, "That should tell you something. Our kids are worried. This has gone too far. We have to do the right thing."

Irritation filled Colleen with tension. "I have not and will not change my mind. We've had this discussion already. There is absolutely nothing to be gained by rehashing it."

"You're wrong, Colleen," Helen said tiredly. "You're making a mistake. We can't keep this secret any longer. It's bigger than we are. When the kids were small it didn't matter, but now they're adults. We can't pretend it never happened."

A mixture of dread and fear crept into Colleen's bones, making her already faulty heart ache. "We can and we will. I will not spend my final days on this earth with my son thinking any differently about me than he does now."

"We were wrong then, we're wrong now," Helen said simply. "We have to make this right."

"Never, do you hear me, Helen McCormick?" Colleen warned. "I won't allow it." A new thought occurred to her. "Besides, there's another side to this situation now."

"What do you mean?"

"I think Zach and Beth are...involved," she offered for lack of a better term.

Helen looked taken aback. The exact same reaction Colleen'd had last night.

"Why would you think that? They've been friends—brother and sister practically—all their lives."

"Be that as it may," Colleen countered. "I know what I saw. And there was absolutely nothing brotherly about the way my son kissed your daughter last night."

Helen's eyes rounded. "Zach kissed Beth?"

"Well, Beth started it. She kissed him first."

"No," Helen denied, a strange look claimed her features, not quite approval, but not quite disapproval.

Colleen sipped her tea in an effort to appear unaffected. "It was a rather stimulating sight. They looked good together."

Helen frowned. "I guess I thought that would never happen."

"With Zach's ambitious drive, I was beginning to wonder if he'd ever settle down."

"We may be reading too much into this," Helen tossed out. "It might just be a passing fancy. You know the ink on Beth's divorce is barely dry."

"But you said yourself she admitted the marriage had been over for years, so it's not like she's on the rebound," Colleen argued.

"And you said," Helen returned, "that Zach went through women—not that I'm speaking ill of him, mind you—like he went through legal briefs, thoroughly but quickly."

Colleen inclined her head in a semblance of a shrug. "It's true. That sweet little receptionist at the Colby Agency, Amy Wells, keeps me informed. He never dates the same woman more than three times."

"Well, he is a very handsome and charming man," Helen admitted. "And busy. I'm sure it's difficult to hold his interest."

"I doubt that's the problem at all," Colleen defended. "I think he has secretly always wanted Beth and that no other woman has ever measured up."

Worry flickered in Helen's eyes. "You don't think he'd *date* Beth three times and then just..."

Colleen shook her head adamantly. "I don't believe he would ever hurt Beth. I won't believe it." She cocked an eyebrow. "If he did there'd be hell to pay, let me tell you."

"They're both adults, it's out of our hands anyway."

"I swear, Helen, you're such a fuddy-duddy. There are things we can do to help them along. I kept her marital woes from Zach just like you asked me, but you should have seen the look on his face the other day when I told him that Beth had left her husband months ago. Besides, it's not like matching the two has never crossed our minds before."

"That was just talk, and it was a long time ago. Things change." She pressed Colleen with a pointed look. "People change."

"You're not going to change my mind," Colleen said, her words final. "Considering this new development I'd think you wouldn't want to risk upsetting the apple cart. Imagine how Beth would feel if she found out the truth? Everything she believes about hers and Zach's relationship would come into question."

Colleen experienced another trickle of relief. She'd gotten through with that one. Helen's adamant expression faltered. Thank Heaven. Maybe now Helen would see things her way.

"I still believe that carrying on with this secret is a mistake," Helen said finally, but her tone didn't sound nearly as convinced.

"But," Colleen interjected, "are you willing to risk your daughter's heart?"

The silence that followed proved telling.

"AT LEAST they're talking," Beth murmured as she peered toward the mezzanine. From where she and Zach stood in the bar they could see the two perfectly, but their mothers couldn't see them.

"It was a little tense for a moment there," Zach commented. "But I knew Mother would never allow a scene in this ritzy joint. She knows that anything she says and does here will end up in the county paper, not to mention be the talk of the town for months to come.''

Beth nodded her agreement. She tried to ignore that he stood so close. She could practically feel his husky voice rumble from his chest. He'd moved up behind her to watch the exchange between their mothers and Beth had struggled to manage even a shallow breath. Having him so close—knowing he knew what she wanted—made her giddy.

Her body heated instantly at the memory of last night's encounter by the oak. All she had to do was close her eyes and she could imagine all over again the feel of his hard body pressed against hers so intimately. His kiss made her want to weep for more. Zach Ashton had definitely mastered the art of kissing. A renewed wave of need washed over her, making her want to lean against him now.

Could she really do this and remain detached emotionally? Every fiber of her being cried out for him…on more than a mere physical level. The notion that she might not be able to keep this just physical, scared her. But not enough so to deter her. She'd made up her mind. She was going to have Zach. If it was a mistake, then so be it. She would not back out now.

He'd known she would have second thoughts. That's why he'd told her if she changed her mind it would be okay with him. She was a *good girl*. He expected her to back out.

A jolt of fury pumped up her resolve. She would go through with it all right. Nothing would stop her. Not even Zach.

"So." He braced his hands on the bar on either side of her and leaned in even closer, his lips only a whisper from her cheek. "Have you had time to think about us?"

Beth couldn't prevent a shiver at the feel of his breath on her skin. His body touched hers now, only the slightest pressure, but the contact was complete from shoulder to thigh. The subtle friction between his silk trousers and shirt and her cotton blouse and skirt made her want to strip off right there and climb inside all that designer silk to feel his naked skin against hers.

"You started this. Now you're going to have to finish it," he murmured huskily.

One arm slid around her waist, his palm flattened on her abdomen and anchored her more fully to him. Beth almost moaned at the pleasure cascading over her. Just like last night, she felt on fire. Would making love with him be this powerful? How would she ever tolerate the intensity?

It was now or never. He was waiting for her answer.

Her pager chirped, startling her. "I have to get that," she mumbled, her voice thick with the slow burn of lust.

Zach eased away from her, but only far enough so that she could dig around in her purse. He had no intention of releasing her from his sensual hold just yet.

Beth checked the display of her pager and almost felt relieved. "I have to get back to the hospital. Sorry," she offered with feigned contrition as she turned to look up at him. Reality had just crashed in on her and she was definitely suffering from cold feet. Those analyzing blue eyes didn't help. She'd seriously underestimated Zach's power over her. She would never in a million years be able to make love with him and simply walk away as if it had never happened. And she had a bad feeling that their coming together would not alleviate in any way her obsession with him. She was sunk.

He smiled. One of those true Ashton charmers. Her heart reacted. ''Give me an answer and I'll let you be on your way,'' he teased gently.

But if the look in his eyes was any indication, he wasn't teasing at all. He wanted an answer. Now. She shouldn't do this. But she couldn't back out. That's what he expected her to do. She didn't want to be just the good little girl next door anymore. She thought about the tattoo parlor and how she'd vowed that she was going to change her image where Zach was concerned.

''Tomorrow night,'' she blurted, then composed herself and added, ''I'm not on call tomorrow night. How about we get together then?'' She gestured toward the mezzanine where their mothers were, from all appearances, enjoying a leisurely lunch. ''They have their weekly card game, so there won't be anyone around to interrupt.''

He looked thoughtful. ''You think they'll go under the circumstances?''

Beth managed a smile at that question. ''Are you kidding? They haven't missed a card game in over ten years. I'm not sure even an act of God would keep them away from the game. Last week your mother beat the pants off the mayor's wife. My mother raved about it for days. They won't miss it.''

That intense gaze focused fully onto hers once more. "Your place or mine?"

Beth thought about that for a moment. As much as she'd always dreamed of finding herself in Zach's bed...she wasn't sure she was ready to go that far just yet.

"My place," she said with a great deal more bravado than she felt. He smiled that pulse-tripping gesture that was pure charm again. She felt the answering flip-flop in her chest.

"I'll bring the wine." With one finger he traced the line of her jaw, lingered near her mouth.

"I'll see you then." Beth slid from between him and the bar and rushed away without looking back.

Twenty-four hours would never be enough time to prepare for the moment she'd spent a lifetime anticipating.

Chapter Seven

Wiping the sweat from his brow, Zach stood back and admired his handiwork. Despite all the mishaps, the gazebo looked pretty good. And not one drop of white paint marred the lush green foliage around it. He couldn't say the same for the first set of clothes he'd worn. He wiped his hands on the rag hanging from his waist and shook his head at the realization of how clumsy he'd been all day.

Sleep hadn't come until the wee hours of the morning. Thoughts of Beth and their *appointment* tonight kept him too wired up to even think about sleep. At the crack of dawn he'd been out pounding the trail around the east side of the property. Though he hadn't crossed paths with Beth, he had taken another fall. He just couldn't understand it. He never missed a step.

He ran a hand through his hair and rotated his left shoulder. He grimaced when it still ached. He hadn't recovered from his first fall. Good thing this morning's tumble hadn't done any additional damage—other than to his pride. And if that wasn't bad enough, he'd barely saved the boxwoods around the gazebo from a whitewashing. He'd grabbed back the unbalanced, half-empty gallon of paint just before it fell off the ladder. In his haste, the can had over-turned in his arms and poured out its contents on him.

Somehow, in spite of his preoccupation with his tempting neighbor, he'd managed to finish the job. Zach checked his watch. He had just enough time for a hot shower and a quick dinner before his mother left for her card game.

He turned and peered across the east garden and to the cottage. Beth had come home about twenty minutes ago. She'd waved, making his heartbeat accelerate. He'd waved back, and almost fallen off the ladder in the process. Lucky for him, she hadn't seemed to notice.

God, he hadn't behaved this ineptly since junior high when he'd stolen his first kiss from Sandy Martin. He was too old to be experiencing this kind of giddiness. Way too old.

But, then, this was Beth. And he'd waited a very long time to be with her like this.

If he wasn't able to stop this thing building between them, would he be able to get on with his life afterward? Or would making love to her bind him further to her?

"The gazebo looks better than it has in years."

He turned at the sound of his mother's voice, and smiled.

"You've done a fabulous job. Your father would be proud."

"Thanks." He knew his mother still missed his dad. Truth be told, he did as well. At least they still had each other.

A small frown furrowed her forehead. "I still can't

imagine why you bothered with it when Hank would have been happy to take care of it.''

"Then I wouldn't have enjoyed all this fresh air and sun,'' Zach countered. He grinned at his mother. Even at a few days shy of seventy-five she looked both attractive and elegant. The turquoise shell and slacks lent color to her pale complexion. Time had turned her auburn hair a shade of gray that most women bought in a bottle. Her silver eyes were clear and left no doubt of the sharp mind behind them.

"I thought that morning ritual of running offered you all the fresh air you needed,'' she suggested with blatant distaste. "I'll never understand what it is with you young people and all that running.'' She eyed him skeptically. "Why, when I was your age the only running I did was after you.''

Zach grinned. "Dad always said I was a handful as a kid.''

"Indeed.'' She patted his arm. "You had to know what every little thing was about. You'd climb anything, eat anything and take apart whatever you got your hands on.''

"I was curious,'' he said with a chuckle.

"I suppose that's what makes you such a good attorney.''

"Ambition?'' he asked.

"That, too,'' she said, "but, in my estimation, what makes you the best is your burning desire to take things apart and find out what makes them tick.''

She had him there. "I'll take that as a compliment.''

She smiled fondly, remembering. "You kept us on our toes. Why I wouldn't have survived the terrible twos if Helen hadn't helped me." Her smile dimmed considerably.

"I'm glad the two of you enjoyed your lunch yesterday," he said sheepishly. He'd taken great care to avoid his mother the rest of the day and evening yesterday. This was the first time they'd had a chance to talk. She'd most likely let him have it now that he'd brought the subject up.

"Why wouldn't we?" she retorted as if she had no idea what he meant.

He shrugged, suppressing a wince when pain jabbed his left shoulder. "It's just that the two of you have been on the outs for days and it was nice to see you together for a change."

"See hear, Zacharius Ashton, I am not a child and neither is Helen. Just because we don't see eye to eye on an issue and aren't speaking doesn't mean we're not still friends. You let us work out our problems in our own time. We don't need you and Beth interfering," she chastised none too gently.

Zach held up his hands in a defensive manner. "We just didn't want you two going for days without speaking," he offered with sincere contrition.

"We speak when there's a need," she informed him. "This will blow over just as soon as Helen sees reason."

He considered that hell could freeze over before that happened. Helen was just about as stubborn as Colleen was. "Point taken. We won't interfere again."

"Speaking of Beth," his mother ventured. "I think this divorce agrees with her. She looks fabulous. Helen says the phone rings all the time." Colleen leaned toward him with a covert look left and right. "She can't believe how many of those young, good-looking doctors are after her daughter. I told her she'd better wise up. Beth is a beautiful woman, one of the brightest doctors on staff at Cartersville General. Lawrence, the administrator—you remember, Lawrence Wallingsford, don't you, Zach? He used to head up the clinic in town when you were in high school."

Ire kindled in Zach's gut. "Sure, I remember him." He didn't want to hear about how many guys were chasing Beth. She hadn't mentioned any significant others. The bottom line was he didn't want to think about her with another man. *He* was going to have her tonight. Dammit he wasn't supposed to be thinking that way either.

"Well—" Colleen darted another of those covert looks toward the cottage as if Helen or Beth might overhear her. "Lawrence said that Beth is a phenomenal doctor and that they'll do anything they have to in order to keep her on staff." She made a knowing sound. "Why, it would please Lawrence to no end if Beth married one of those nice young men from the Cartersville area. What better way to keep her around?"

A buzzing began in Zach's ears. Fury burst inside him like shattering glass. He didn't give one damn what Lawrence whoever wanted. He was going to have Beth and no one—*no one*—else was going to get in his way.

"If you'll excuse me, Mother, I have to hit the shower."

Colleen watched her son storm toward the back door. She smiled a secret smile.

Mission accomplished.

BETH SMOOTHED a hand over her very short, very black sheath. It was the shortest, slinkiest dress she'd ever owned. The woman in the boutique had insisted that it was the kind of thing that drove men crazy. Beth turned and glanced over her shoulder to view the back. Her helpful sales associate had also insisted that this sort of dress could not be worn over anything other than thong panties, if any were worn at all. Beth felt a flush of embarrassment even now. Never, not once in her life, had she ever had a conversation like that with her closest confidant, much less a stranger.

She supposed it was a good thing she'd already bought the proper undies. At least it saved her from having to allow the woman to go into a detailed explanation of which brand was the most comfortable. To Beth's way of thinking, none of them would be. Certainly not the minuscule black things she was wearing at the moment.

Facing the mirror once more, she stared at her reflection for a long time trying to decide if she was happy with what she saw. Not the dress, or her upswept hairdo, but with what she saw in her eyes.

This was what she wanted. Her heart skipped a beat for emphasis. Whether it was right or wrong or would change anything—for better or worse—she wanted this night with Zach more than she wanted to take her next breath. She wanted to make that connection with him...to see if it would be all that she'd dreamed it could be.

She shook her head at her foolish musings and turned her attention to her room. Slowly, she scrutinized the preparations she'd made. She'd hidden away the mementos of her high school and college days. Her mother had insisted on keeping them out all these years. But now that Beth lived here again, she'd just as soon forget about that little girl from the past. She'd replaced the items with certificates and acknowledgments from her profession.

A few pictures, mostly of her mother and father, some with her in them as well, were scattered about. The shades behind the lace curtains were drawn. The bed was freshly made with clean linens. She'd tossed the throw pillows around on the comforter to make it look less like she'd just made it. Scented candles flickered on the bedside table, gifting the room with delicate, sensuous fragrances.

Beth looked at the digital clock and gasped. He'd be here any minute. Her nerves jangling, she repositioned the pillows, then changed them yet again when she wasn't quite satisfied. She scanned her reflection one more time and decided the silver dangly earrings had to go. Instead, she selected a delicate pearl set that looked a lot less flashy. She surveyed herself one last time and every ounce of her courage drained away.

"I can't do this," she told the uncertain woman in the mirror.

What was she thinking wearing a dress like this? And G-string underwear? She flung her closet door open and shuffled through the hangers. There had to be something else she could change into before he arrived. Anything would be better than this. What a foolish idea! She had to be losing her mind to behave so…so out of character.

The doorbell chimed.

Beth's heart skipped, sending her pulse into an erratic staccato. She slammed her closet door shut and leaned against it. If she didn't answer, he'd go away. He would give up and walk back across the garden to his own house.

But you've waited for this since you were fourteen, another voice intruded. You can't let this moment pass. You've got to do it. Beth swallowed, then licked her suddenly dry lips. She was dressed. Her room looked better than it had in years. It smelled wonderful. There were condoms of all kinds on the bedside table next to the candles.

He probably carried his own condoms.

The bell chimed again.

Beth raced to the bedside table and jerked the drawer open so she could sweep the condoms into it. She slammed it shut.

"Okay." She squared her shoulders and took a deep bolstering breath. "Time to put your money where your mouth is, McCormick."

Tension rolling over her in waves, Beth walked slowly, each step deliberately measured, toward the front door. Her mother was at her weekly card game. Thankfully she hadn't complained too much about yesterday's surprise luncheon. Though Helen seemed considerably more relaxed where the dispute between her and Colleen was concerned, she did stare rather strangely at Beth. She had insisted that it was nothing, but Beth knew that look. She remembered it from the day when she'd been twelve and she'd had to be rushed to the hospital with a broken arm. Her mother was worried about her for some reason.

Beth couldn't fathom what her concern might be. Maybe she'd ask her again tonight after she came home. Beth stalled a few feet from the front door. She hadn't stopped to think that her mother would be coming home, shortly before midnight if the game played out as usual. What would she do...?

Zach would just have to go home before her mother returned. Though she was thirty-one, her mother was still her mother.

The bell chimed for the fourth time. Beth stared at the door and told herself one last time that she could do this. Her fists clenching and unclenching she took the final steps, closed her right hand around the knob and opened the door.

Those breaths she'd had difficulty achieving, ceased altogether when her gaze landed on the man at her door. He looked amazing. Navy trousers and a paler blue shirt fit his body as if they were tailor made for him, which they probably were, and enhanced the heart-stopping blue of his eyes. His hair was combed back, except for one errant lock that spilled across his forehead. His chiseled jaw was clean shaven, and that smile on his full lips would have made a nun rescind her vows.

"You look terrific," he said, his own tone a little breathless. He held up a bottle and two wineglasses. "I have the refreshments."

"Come in." Beth reminded herself to step back so that he could enter. Speech proved even more troublesome than breathing. She closed her eyes and counted to three in hopes of pulling herself together by blocking all stimuli.

It didn't help.

He was perfect. Everything she'd ever hoped for and dreamed of. The one man who had haunted her for as long as she could remember. Zach had always been her everything. Her protector, her friend, her soul mate. But he'd always held one part of his life back. The sexual side. Tonight that was going to change. Tonight was the night.

"Living room?" he asked when she failed to gather her wits and show him to a room. "Or straight to your room?"

She dredged up a tight smile. "Living room."

He followed her down the short entry hall and into the living room. She'd made a few adjustments in here as well. The one family photo that included her ex-husband was tucked away in a drawer. Her favorite soft rock CD played softly in the background. Everything was just exactly as it should be...

Except her. She was a tangle of nerves.

Zach sat the glasses and the sweating bottle of chilled wine on the coffee table.

"Oh!" Beth jerked into hostess mode. "Do you need—" Before she could finish her sentence he had pulled a corkscrew from his back pocket. "Guess not," she mumbled.

He uncorked the bottle and set it aside. His attention moved immediately back to her.

"You really look great." His gaze traveled over her slowly, thoroughly. "Is that a new dress?"

She started to nod but caught herself. "I've had it for years," she lied.

He inclined his head and took his time studying her once more. "I'm glad you chose to wear it tonight." He poured a glass of wine, the sound echoed around her, making her shiver. He offered her the glass. "I selected this just for you."

"Thank you." She took a sip of the pale gold liquid and smiled. "It's wonderful."

He filled the remaining glass. "It's sweet and too good to have any other way but alone."

She took another gulp of her wine. There was that word again: *good*. Why did he always have to associate good with her? Yes, she was good, but she was a lot of other things, too. Like a woman who has decided what she wants and is determined to have it.

"It is sweet," was all she said. She downed the rest and held out her glass for more. He obliged.

The old family photographs on the mantel captured his attention as he sat the bottle back down. Beth sipped her second glass as he crossed the room to look at them. She had to calm down and pull herself together. Here she stood, in the middle of the room, gulping wine as if she were scared to death.

The hell of it was, she was scared to death.

Beth finished off her glass and ordered herself to calm down.

She could do this...she *would* do this.

She'd only regret it for the rest of her life if she didn't. Zach was apparently willing and she might never have this chance again.

"This is a great picture of your father," Zach commented. "Hey, remember the day he let me take you to the carnival in Cartersville." He laughed, remembering. "You wanted to go so bad and your mother was dead set against it."

"So Dad allowed you to take me and never told Mom," she finished for him.

Zach turned to her and smiled. "We had a great time, didn't we?"

He'd liked playing big brother to her. But she wasn't his sister, and she definitely wasn't a kid anymore.

"We did," she agreed. She felt much calmer now.

The wine was doing its work, sending its warmth all through her.

He just looked at her then, searching her eyes, waiting. Then he spoke, "You're sure this is what you want?"

Fury whipped through her. She plunked her glass down on the nearest table and planted her hands on her hips. "I don't believe this," she hissed. "Now is not the time to ask me if this is what I want. Isn't it clear?" She glared at the floor in an effort to drag her temper back down to a controllable level. "I swear, Zach, what do I have to do to convince you that I'm not a little girl anymore?"

He was standing right next to her when she looked up. She gasped, barely catching herself before she drew back a step.

"I can see that you're no little girl. That's not the issue," he said gently. One finger traced a path down her bare arm. "You mean a great deal to me, Beth. There has only been one other woman who held a place in my heart before and after an affair, Alex Preston. She's with the agency, too. We're friends...good friends. The women I prefer in bed are not generally the same ones with whom I have other relationships."

Alex Preston. Jealousy slid through Beth making her want to claw the eyes out of a woman she'd never even met.

Fortified with wine and fury, Beth glowered at him. "Are you saying that you think I'm not woman enough for you? Is that it? A good girl like me couldn't possibly do the job right?"

"That's not what I'm saying."

She grabbed him by the shirtfront, pulled him

down to her and kissed him hard on the mouth, then released him.

"Never judge a book by its cover, Zach." She lifted her chin a notch, daring him. "You might be surprised at what I can do."

He grabbed her this time. His mouth came down on hers with crushing intensity. His arms clamped around her like a vice, molding her softness to his muscular contours. She could feel every hard ripple and bulge. His tongue thrust into her mouth at the same time that his hands slid over her bottom and pulled her against his hips. She moaned her approval, helpless to do anything but cling to him.

When his fingers slipped beneath the hem and discovered the bare skin of her bottom, he groaned his own satisfaction. Lost to the desire singing through her veins, Beth could only whimper when he scooped her into his arms and strode toward her room. He kicked the door closed behind them, his mouth still punishing hers with a sensual roughness.

When her feet were on the floor once more, his hands were already on the zipper of her dress. He kissed her throat now, hot, lingering kisses that made her blood boil. The dress eased off her shoulders and slid down her body, the silk making her skin tingle.

His mouth followed the descent of the flimsy fabric. He paused to admire her breasts, his warm breath sending hot, licking flames of desire coursing over her. Her nipples jutted out for his attention and when he'd had his fill of looking, he took one in his mouth. She cried out her pleasure as he dropped to his knees, his mouth and fingers working magic on her aching breasts. Her own fingers threaded into his silky hair, urging on his delicious ministrations.

Then he moved lower.

Beth stopped breathing. She wasn't sure she could live through this exquisite torture. His mouth and tongue laved her skin, pausing at strategic spots to nuzzle and pay special attention. His fingers kneaded her bare bottom, adding another layer of sensation.

He suddenly stopped.

Beth almost cried out.

She could feel his ragged breath against the skin he'd so thoroughly moistened and sensitized with his mouth and tongue. His hands stilled on her hips.

Wanting more, she looked down at him to find out why he'd stopped. He was staring at her belly button. Or, more accurately, at her belly button ring. The one she'd gotten at the tattoo parlor.

He lifted his gaze to hers, his expression unreadable.

He didn't like it. Dread pooled in her stomach. She shouldn't have—

A devilish smile slid across that masterful mouth. "Oh, baby, you do have a wicked side."

A tiny smile tugged at her lips. "You don't know the half of it."

His gaze still on hers, he stood. He pulled the pins from her hair and allowed it to fall around her shoulders. Then, while they stared into each other's eyes, he opened his shirt, one button at a time. He drew out each step, making her wait. Making her want to beg for him to hurry.

Finally, the shirt drifted to the floor. The air that had only just started filling her lungs once more caught as her hands flattened against his beautiful chest. He stood, frozen, while she smoothed her palms over him…the way she'd dreamed of doing for so very long.

Way before she'd had her fill, he lifted her against him once more. As he moved toward the bed she kicked off her shoes. Pushing aside the pillows she'd so strategically placed, he laid her gently on the soft comforter. He kissed her, tenderly this time, his powerful body hovering over hers. When his mouth left hers, he stood next to the bed and unfastened his belt…reached for his fly—

Her pager sounded off like a siren, shattering the sweet silence.

She reached for it, the move second nature, and read the display. The hospital. Snatching up the receiver, she focused on slowing her respiration while she punched in the numbers.

"I thought you weren't on call tonight," he said, sitting down on the bed beside her.

Was that disappointment she heard in his voice? "I'm not. But Helen or Colleen could have been in an accident."

The information relayed to her made her heart squeeze in her chest. It wasn't their mothers, it was Laurie Ellroy. She'd been rushed to the emergency room an hour or so ago, and now she was being admitted.

Beth had no choice.

She hung up the receiver.

"I have to go." She looked up at Zach and wished she could stay. He looked magnificent. Her body ached in protest of what she knew she had to do.

"I understand." He stood and turned toward her door.

Just when she thought he was going to walk out,

he bent down and picked up her dress. He brought it to her, then rounded up her shoes. Touched by his thoughtfulness, Beth scrambled off the bed and into her dress. He zipped it for her while she held her hair out of the way.

"I'm sorry," she offered. "This patient isn't even mine anymore...not technically. But I promised her mother that I would be there for them." She turned to Zach and prayed he would somehow understand how difficult this was, both leaving him and knowing Laurie was worse. "I really am sorry," she repeated.

He brushed a wisp of hair from her cheek. "Don't be. I can take a rain check. If this patient needs you, you should go. Call me when you get back."

Stepping into her shoes, it hit her that she'd had two glasses of wine only minutes ago. She swore softly.

"What's wrong?" Unlike before, his fingers were making quick work of buttoning his shirt.

"The wine. I probably shouldn't even be driving," she fretted. "But I have to go."

In five seconds flat he was tucked in and buttoned down. "I'll drive you." He smiled. "After all, I'm the one who brought the wine."

She made a distressed face. "I can't be sure how long I'll be there."

He shrugged. "They still keep magazines in the waiting rooms, don't they?"

Beth didn't argue any further. She had to go, and, she admitted, she was glad he was going with her.

At least they would be together. And that suddenly meant a great deal to her.

ZACH FOLLOWED Beth down the long, sixth floor corridor. His stomach had tightened instantly at the smell upon entering the place. A dozen memories of sitting by his father's bedside while the life drained from him overwhelmed Zach. He didn't like hospitals. Then again, he countered, pushing away thoughts of death and dying, who did? He watched Beth's purposeful strides as he considered his question. He supposed doctors and nurses did. Or maybe they just felt compelled to do their work with no concern as to where it was performed. He had a feeling that Beth cared deeply for her work. And she was good. He knew it without his mother having told him what the hospital administrator had to say.

How many doctors would rush to a hospital to hold the hand of a patient that wasn't even hers any longer?

Not many, he felt certain.

Beth had explained on the way that this twenty-two-year-old woman had leukemia. She needed a bone marrow donor or she would die. The mother's own health problems prevented her from being a suitable donor. The father was dead and the girl had no siblings. Regret twisted in his stomach at the thought of such a tragic waste. The patient had just graduated from college, according to Beth, and would have started her first teaching job this fall had fate not played such a dirty trick on her.

''Dr. Daniels!'' A feminine voice called out from the nurse's station.

Zach slowed, allowing Beth to go ahead of him. The woman, who looked to be in her fifties, threw her arms around Beth. He resisted the urge to frown at the woman's use of Beth's married name. He wondered why she would want to retain her ex's name.

Could there be something between them still? Irritation, fierce and unreasonable, tightened his jaw.

"I'm so sorry I had to call you."

Beth drew back to look at her. "Don't even think about leaving me out. I told you to call me. I'd be very disappointed if you didn't."

The woman nodded, tears brimming in her eyes. "She's better now. Sleeping." She sighed. "I was just going to have them call you and tell you not to come."

"It wouldn't have done any good," Beth told her. "I would have come anyway. Can I get you anything?"

The older woman swiped her cheeks and managed a smile. "No, no. I'm all right."

"You've eaten?"

The woman nodded. Zach noticed how thin and tired she looked. But then he imagined that watching one's child die would do that to a person. That and much worse, he added, that sick feeling rising in his gut again.

The woman looked over Beth's shoulder and caught a glimpse of Zach, then she took in Beth's appearance a little more closely. As if she'd just deduced what she may have interrupted, her hand flew to her mouth then fluttered in the air. "I am so sorry. You shouldn't have come."

"Oh, gosh," Beth said, color tingeing her cheeks as she realized her oversight. "I forgot all about you, Zach." She ushered the woman toward him. "Jenny Ellroy, this is Zach."

Zach nodded an acknowledgment. "It's a pleasure to meet you, ma'am. I'm very sorry about...the circumstances."

A frown etching its way across her features, the woman extended her hand. "You look so familiar." Her frown deepened. "Are you from Cartersville?"

He took her hand and shook it gently. "Zach Ashton," he told her. "I was raised in Kelso. It's not far from here."

"Ashton?" she echoed.

The color drained from her face right before Zach's eyes. He was certain she would have swayed had it not been for Beth's arm around her shoulders.

"I think you need to sit down," Beth offered. "Let's get you back to Laurie's room."

The woman nodded distractedly, her gaze never leaving Zach. He wasn't sure what he should do or say. Maybe all the stress from her daughter's illness had suddenly hit her.

He followed Beth and Jenny into a room four doors down from the nurse's station. He felt a little uncomfortable in a stranger's hospital room, but the girl was sleeping so she would never know. While Beth situated the mother in a chair near the bedside table, Zach took in the features of the daughter. She looked extremely pale. The color of her skin was parchment white, a sharp contrast to her dark hair. Like her mother, she appeared to be rail thin. And so very, very young. She looked like a child rather than a recent college graduate. What a terrible waste. Surely a donor would be found.

"Zach," Beth whispered from right beside him.

He tried not to show how much she'd startled him. "Yeah?"

"Would you go down to the cafeteria and get Mrs. Ellroy a cup of black coffee and something sweet. A doughnut , maybe. She needs a little perking up."

He nodded. "Sure." He glanced in the woman's direction and was surprised to find her still staring at him. Her strange preoccupation with him didn't really make him uncomfortable. It did, however, concern him. Had his presence added a strain to an already stressful situation?

"I'll be right back," he told Beth. "Then maybe I should hang out in the waiting room."

Before Beth could say anything, Mrs. Ellroy leaned forward. "Please," she whispered just loud enough for him to hear. "Please, don't go."

Chapter Eight

By 2:00 a.m. Zach had seen a great deal more suffering than he'd wanted to. The young girl, Laurie, had awoken suddenly and all hell had broken loose. Between the bouts of vomiting and plummets in her blood pressure, the girl had scared the wits out of most of the staff working her case. The oncologist had finally arrived and things had calmed down.

Though Zach was no stranger to suffering, he'd watched his father die an excruciatingly slow death with cancer, this was somehow different. When his father had died, he'd been sixty-five years old—still too young to die by any standards—but watching a girl so painfully young that she'd barely tasted life hang on by a mere thread was almost more than Zach could take. It made him ponder the unfairness of life more deeply than he ever had before.

The one bright spot had been watching Beth. She was utterly amazing. Her burning desire to help was so clear. She was relentless. Every moment, every breath she took was focused on her patient and the patient's mother. He couldn't see how anyone could lose hope with Beth on her side. Her steady reassurances and enthusiasm under fire were a credit to her professional ability. He could definitely understand why the hospital wanted to keep her.

Just another reason *they* could never be. She was needed here. She obviously loved her job. And Zach loved his job back in Chicago. Though he certainly couldn't claim the healing and life-saving skills Beth offered to her patients, he was very good at what he did. Victoria Colby told him time and again how she couldn't manage without him. And he could never be the kind of attorney who sorted out divorce cases or drew up last wills and testaments for his clients.

Laurie was resting again by 2:30 a.m. Even Zach felt grateful. Maybe her mother could get some badly needed rest now. Zach waited near the door while Beth said her goodbyes. Though she wasn't on duty, she insisted she'd be back later in the day to check on Laurie.

The final, beseeching look Mrs. Ellroy focused on him shifted something in his chest. He couldn't say what it was exactly, but he felt something for her. Sympathy, maybe? He offered her a smile and that seemed to placate the expectant look in her eyes.

"I'm sorry I kept you here so long," Beth murmured as they walked in the direction of the elevator bank on the sixth floor. She sounded exhausted.

"It wasn't a problem." Instinctively he placed his hand at the small of her back for comfort. "I'm glad I had the opportunity to see you in action."

One of the nurses called goodbye to Beth as they passed the nurse's station. The elevators were located at the far end of the corridor where this new wing connected with the original structure. When they reached their destination Zach pressed the call button.

Beth looked at him for a time before she finally spoke again. "Tonight was one of the less pleasant aspects of being a physician."

"You handled it extremely well."

She made a sound that could have been a laugh had it not been entirely humorless and far too dry. "But it's not enough."

The elevator doors opened and they stepped inside. Both remained silent as it glided into downward motion, then bumped to a stop on the lobby level.

"Maybe they'll find a donor soon," he offered when they'd exited the building.

"We can hope," she replied, her tone lacking optimism.

Zach inhaled deeply of the cool night air, clearing his lungs of the medicinal smell of healing and the underlying stench of death and dying. He'd discovered over the course of the night that the sixth floor of the hospital's new wing was the oncology floor where death loomed among the miracles like a towering hawk ready to swoop down on its victims.

Pushing that harsh reality from his mind, he opened the car door for Beth, but she hesitated and looked up at him. Even in the sparse moonlight and the pale glow from the car's interior lamp, he could see the tears glittering in her eyes.

"I'm sorry things didn't work out tonight, Zach." She moistened her lips and sucked in a shaky breath. "I wanted things to be perfect. I…"

He took her in his arms and held her close.

"I wish…" she sobbed. "I wish I could do something."

He didn't say anything, he just kept holding her against his chest. He knew she wasn't talking about him now or their missed time together. She meant the patient she'd left on the sixth floor. With a fierceness that surprised even him, he wished he could do something, too. But he couldn't. All either of them could do was hope.

Zach had known how selfless Beth was, but now he understood something he hadn't before. Whenever she lost or felt on the verge of losing a patient, she lost a little piece of herself as well. He wanted more than he'd ever wanted anything before to somehow make up for that. To fill in the voids left by the reality of her chosen profession.

To make her whole.

So he stood there, in the near darkness, with the September breeze wafting around them as he held her, and he knew that no matter what happened from this point on there was no turning back for him. He loved Beth. Nothing would ever change that. He would give her whatever she asked of him and then he'd go back to Chicago and leave her here where she was happy…where she belonged. He would never, no matter how much he wanted to, ask her to leave what she loved. Even if she felt the same way about him, he wouldn't ask her to chose.

Marriage wasn't for him anyway. He'd made that decision the day she walked down the aisle with another man. What would he do with a wife and kids? He didn't have time for that kind of life.

She hadn't asked him to marry her anyway, she'd asked him to have an affair with her. Proof positive that she didn't feel the same way he did.

Oh well, he supposed it served him right. He'd broken enough hearts over the years. Time about was fair play, wasn't it?

HELEN POUNDED on Colleen's kitchen door and waited, her patience growing thinner with each passing moment. Finally, Colleen jerked the door open.

"Why on earth are you knocking?" Colleen griped. "You've come in and out of this house at will for over forty years. Why change your routine now? Besides, what could be so all fired important at this hour?"

Helen raised an accusing brow. "It's nine o'clock in the morning. If you haven't gotten your beauty rest by this hour, it ain't happening."

Colleen huffed. "I was not in bed. I was on the telephone if you must know." She swept her arms down the front of her body. "Can you not see that I'm dressed?"

Helen shrugged noncommittally. "It's hard to tell. Some of those fancy duds you wear look just like pajamas."

"Just because you prefer the *rustic* look, doesn't mean I have to," Colleen snapped. "Now, what is it you need?"

Helen held up the two stemmed wineglasses and a corkscrew. "These belong to you, I believe."

Colleen glowered at the items in question. "If they do, you know where they go." She backed up and opened the door wider. "Come in, won't you?" she invited, her tone purposely patronizing.

Aggravated beyond reason, Helen stomped inside. "I found these in my living room along with an opened bottle of wine." She placed the glasses in the dishwasher, and the corkscrew in its proper drawer.

"Really?" Colleen poured herself a cup of coffee. "Want some?" She waggled the half-empty pot at Helen.

Helen shook her head. "Was Zach at home last night?"

Colleen frowned. "Now that you mention it, I don't remember seeing his car in the drive when I came home."

"Beth wasn't home either when I got back from the card game." Setting her coffee aside, Colleen studied Helen with mounting suspicion. "You think they were together."

"I know they were together. Beth came home a few minutes after three. I heard them at the door."

"Then why did you ask me if he was home?" Colleen's eyes suddenly widened with anticipation. "What happened? Did they kiss again?"

Helen wanted to shake her. Couldn't she see what all this would lead to? "All I heard was him say good-night."

"Hmm." Colleen sat down at the table and placed her chin in her hand. A rather unladylike position, but she needed to think at the moment. "Wine...out late together...but they didn't do any smooching at the door..."

"Good grief, Colleen," Helen fired as she dropped into a seat on the opposite side of the table. "These are our children you're talking about."

"Well it's not as if they haven't already done it with other people. You should be glad they're attracted to each other. I can't imagine a woman I'd be more pleased to have as my daughter-in-law."

Helen rolled her eyes. "That's not the point. I love Zach as if he were my own, but this could be wrong for both of them."

Colleen leaned forward slightly and fixed her with

a hard look. "Don't even think about bringing up the other thing. I'll leave the room if you do."

"Putting *that* aside," Helen went on, "Beth's work is here, Zach's is in Chicago. One of them will have to compromise. And I don't think it will ever work. Beth had her fill of city life in Indianapolis. She's told me several times how glad she is to be back here at a smaller hospital. And I'm sure Zach would never want to return to Kelso permanently. He seems to love his work in Chicago."

"There are small, private hospitals in Chicago," Colleen countered. "Why wouldn't Beth be happy at one of them?"

Helen shrugged. "The only way we would know the answer to that question is if she were asked."

Colleen looked thoughtful. Dread trickled through Helen. She knew that look. Colleen was devising a plan. Helen stood, determined not to be a part of her old friend's machinations this time.

"And I've made a decision about us," Helen announced as an afterthought.

Her words dragged Colleen's attention back to the conversation. "You have?"

"I've decided that I'm not going to fight with you anymore over the issue."

Colleen's expectant gaze narrowed with suspicion. "Why?"

Helen played her trump car. "Because I trust you. I don't know why I've been such a bear about the whole thing when I know perfectly well that in the end you'll do what's right. That's the kind of person you are." With that said, she turned and walked out.

Colleen stared after Helen. The nerve of the woman! Did she really believe such a thing? Colleen could feel her blood pressure rising. She forced away thoughts of Helen and her latest declaration. Colleen didn't need any more stress, besides she had bigger fish to fry.

Now, who did she know in Chicago...

A DISTANT RINGING tugged Beth from her deep slumber. Reluctant to rouse from her dreams of making love with Zach, she opened her eyes a fraction at a time. His scent filled her nostrils and she smiled. She hugged the dress she'd worn last night a little closer and inhaled deeply of Zach's arousing scent. He'd held her close for a very long time this morning, comforting her in a completely nonsexual manner. His subtle aftershave and a hint of his own unique fragrance clung to the silk garment she'd worn. After he'd gone home, she'd fallen into bed, completely exhausted, the dress tucked next to her pillow. If she couldn't have the real thing at least she could dream of him.

Another ring jolted her fully awake. The source of the sound finally penetrated the remaining layer of sleep enshrouding her. The telephone. She squinted at the digital clock—9:20 a.m. Too early considering she hadn't made it to bed until after three. Groaning with displeasure she reached for the phone. She dragged the receiver from its cradle on her bedside table and managed a thick hello.

"Beth, Mayor Chadwick here."

Another groan almost escaped her. "Good morning, Mayor." She eased up on one elbow. "What can I do for you today?" Like she didn't know. She'd tried her level best not to think about that darned birthday celebration the past couple of days.

She supposed she couldn't put it off any longer. With only one week to go until show time, she had no choice. It was time to suck it up and get what she had to do done.

"We've started on the floats for the parade, but I wanted you to have the final say on what we've come up with for Colleen. Is it possible for you to come down to the granary warehouse this morning and take a look at what we're doing?"

Beth sat up and shoved the hair back from her face. She moistened her dry lips. "Sure, I'll be right there." She estimated she could shower and dress and drive into town in thirty minutes. That should be soon enough.

"Have you given any more thought to that theme?" he ventured. "We thought you might want to tie it in with our float suggestion."

Beth tried to work up a little enthusiasm, but it was slow in coming. "That sounds like a wonderful idea."

"I'll see you shortly then."

Hanging up the receiver Beth considered whether or not she should try and talk her mother into coming with her. Why not? The worst Helen could do was say no.

Three cups of coffee and twenty-five minutes later, Beth was on her way into town with her mother in the passenger seat. Helen had shocked her by offering to go along before Beth even asked. Maybe that luncheon date she and Zach had engineered had done more good than Beth thought. Whatever the case, she was glad to have her mother involved in the activities once more.

When Beth braked to a stop in the parking area

outside the old granary warehouse, Zach's shiny red sports car grabbed her attention. She hadn't considered that he would be here, though she obviously should have. Her gaze went immediately to the rearview mirror where she scrutinized her thrown together appearance. She wore no makeup. Her hair was twisted up and pinned in a loose knot and still wasn't completely dry. Her jeans were worn comfortable and her Hoosiers T-shirt was baggy and faded. She looked completely unkempt.

"You look fine, dear," her mother said, startling Beth who'd somehow forgotten she was even there. "Now come along."

Beth smiled. Of course, she looked fine. It was Saturday. And she'd come prepared to work on the parade floats if needed. "Thanks, Mom." She opened her door and got out, then looked across the top of the car at her mother. "I'm a little out of it this morning. I was at the hospital until two-thirty."

"At the hospital?" Helen sounded surprised.

Frowning, Beth closed her door. "Yes. Where did you think I was?"

Her mother shook her head. "Oh, I hadn't really thought about it. Is everything all right?"

Beth decided her mother averted her gaze far too quickly. Something was up. "One of my patients—well she used to be my patient—had a worrisome reaction to her chemo treatment. I went in to check on her."

"That's too bad." Helen started around the car. "Is she going to be okay?"

Beth rounded the hood and matched her stride to her mother's as they made their way to the warehouse. "Probably not. She needs a bone marrow transplant and the odds of finding a good match are almost nil.'' Beth sighed. ''She's only twenty-two.''

Helen paused before entering the building and met her daughter's gaze. ''That's just awful. Are *you* okay?''

Beth kissed her cheek. ''I'll make it. Thanks for asking.'' Maybe she'd read too much into Helen's actions this morning.

Inside Beth was amazed at the sheer number of volunteers working steadily. Several floats were already taking shape. She almost laughed at the black-and-white cow near the end of the room. It didn't take a rocket scientist to figure out to whom that one belonged. Old Bert was still cashing in on his claim to fame.

''I'm going over to see Viola,'' Helen told her before walking away.

Beth smiled as she surveyed the activities once more. This was one of the things she loved most about small towns. People took the time to show they cared. In the city everyone was too busy. She hadn't even known her own neighbors when she'd lived in Indianapolis. That life wasn't for her.

''Good morning.''

The sound of Zach's husky voice washed over her, triggering an instant surge of desire. ''Good morning,'' she returned.

She tried not to stare at him, but she just couldn't help herself. He looked wonderful, and, to her relief, he was dressed very much as she was. His jeans were every bit as worn as her own, and the Columbia University T-shirt was faded practically beyond recognition. The urge to move closer to him all but overwhelmed her. He drew her on every conscious level, and some she hadn't even known existed until a few days ago. She doubted any other man could make her feel quite this way.

"Any word on Laurie this morning?" His gaze, as well as his voice, turned solemn.

"One of the nurses called about six, right before her shift ended, and told me that Laurie was still resting comfortably. So that's a good sign."

"Until the next time," Zach added somberly.

Beth nodded. Words weren't necessary. Both recognized where Laurie's situation was headed.

"I sent balloons this morning," he said, then looked away. "I hope that's okay."

Beth touched his forearm. It was all she dared do for fear of throwing her arms around him and holding him tight in front of everyone including her mother. But even the small contact of her fingers against his warm skin tugged at her senses in a way that made her weak with need.

"I'm sure Laurie and her mother will appreciate that you were thinking of them."

His gaze leveled on hers once more in a heart-stopping show of blue. "Is it like this often?"

He didn't have to explain what he meant. "Sometimes. But there are enough times in between when we're able to help people that it cushions moments like this."

"But it still hurts," he suggested, his tone too knowing.

"Yes," she admitted. "It still hurts."

He inhaled a big breath. "But you keep doing it anyway, because it's who you are."

She nodded. "Just like you."

For a long time he stood there and simply looked

at her without saying anything. Finally, he spoke, "I realized this morning that you're right where you belong." He opened his arms in a magnanimous, yet seemingly weary manner. "That this is what means the most to you. This place and these people."

Beth read the question in his eyes, but couldn't quite decipher the emotion there. "That's true. This is home."

He sighed just a little. "That's what I thought."

Before she could fathom his intent, he leaned down and kissed her cheek. The brief touch sent her heart racing. Her breath caught during that millisecond when he paused before drawing away. But draw away he did.

"Don't ever let anyone change you," he said, his eyes emphasizing his words.

He didn't give her a chance to respond before he rejoined the planning committee gathered around a large worktable in the center of the room. Beth could only stand there for a minute or so. She scanned the faces around her, all so familiar and so dear. This was home and these people were all part of one big family. She did love it here. Her gaze sought and found Zach. Just as she loved him. She could count on him. He'd always been there for her whenever she needed him. They were more than friends...more than just family.

Their relationship meant far too much to risk it for the sake of a brief affair. No matter how much she wanted him like that, would a few moments of physical satisfaction be worth a lifetime of friendship? She and Matt had been friends all during medical school. And, admittedly, they were still friends now, even after the divorce. But it wasn't quite the same. She regretted that.

She didn't want what she and Zach had to ever fall into that category. So maybe she'd made a mistake. Acted too hastily. An empty feeling welled inside her, creating a sense of loss that echoed to the depths of her soul. A feeling of loss for something she'd never even had.

Zach grinned at something Harve said and Beth's heart reacted. Some things were just better left alone.

"Beth!" Mayor Chadwick called. "Come tell us what you think of this!"

Beth made her way to the worktable where sketches, some rather good, some not, were spread across the top. Her attention focused in on one design in particular. At first she couldn't believe what she was seeing, but on further inspection she knew it was exactly what she thought. An elegant, rose embellished—

"I think it makes the perfect statement," Mayor Chadwick insisted. "A float befitting of the lady to ride upon it."

"It's a throne," Zach said hesitantly, as if he weren't sure everyone else understood what they were looking at.

An honest-to-God throne. Beth still couldn't believe her eyes, even when her ears confirmed it.

"I've thought it all out," the mayor enthused. "Instead of giving her the keys to the city or some such nonsense—everybody and their brother does that old cliché—we'll crown her as Queen of Kelso!"

Beth's gaze collided with Zach's. He adopted a helpless expression. It was his mother, he couldn't exactly protest too loudly.

Still looking at Zach, Beth offered, "Do you think the formality of it might embarrass Mrs. Ashton just a little?"

"She'll love it!" Viola interjected. "Queen for a day."

The mayor chuckled. "Why she'll be thrilled," he added. "You know how Ms. Colleen loves to be the center of attention."

"You're not supposed to encourage her, Arnold," Helen scolded, addressing the mayor by his first name. "Why that's the most ridiculous thing I've ever seen."

"I designed it myself," Viola protested, color darkening her cheeks.

"I wouldn't be bragging about it," Helen retorted, always the paragon of honesty.

Before Viola and Helen could start in on each other, Zach intervened, "I think we should keep it simple." He smiled at Viola. "Though it's a lovely design, how about we tone it down just a smidgen?"

Pouting, Viola sniffed. "I suppose I could scale back on the embellishments."

While they hashed out the design of the float, Beth studied over her initial idea for the theme. Mrs. Ashton had spent a lifetime being a friend to all. Why not focus in on that concept? Maybe the idea would drive home the need for Helen and Colleen to make amends.

"For the theme," Beth cut into the hum of conversation. All eyes turned to her. "I was thinking friendship should be the main focus." Doubt clouded most of their faces. "Think about it," she went on. "Mrs. Ashton has been a friend, offering help anyway she could, to the whole town for most of her adult life. Any one of you could probably come up with your own personal occasion when she helped you in one capacity or another.''

Sounds of agreement rumbled through the gathered crowd. No one could argue with that.

''I like that,'' Zach said. ''What do you think, Mrs. McCormick?''

Helen looked at a loss for words for one long moment. ''That...sounds good. Much better than the queen idea.''

Beth frowned at her mother's apparent reluctance. ''Whatever else happens in our lives, a good friend is priceless,'' she reminded all listening. Her gaze shifted to Zach's and something passed between them. An understanding of sorts that neither of them could deny.

As everyone else in the room latched on to the theme and ran with the concept, Beth kept her gaze locked with Zach's. She knew what she had to do.

If she read him right, he did, too.

Chapter Nine

"Lucy, hey, it's Beth." Beth listened as her friend went through a lengthy but good-natured monologue about how she hated working Saturdays and that Beth should be there to enjoy all the fun. "You can call me in two weeks when I'm at work and you're home," Beth suggested in an effort to placate her. Lucy's answering laugh told her she'd said the right thing. "Look, I wanted to check on the Ellroy girl. How's she doing? I might drop by to see her if she isn't released today."

The news was good. Laurie's vitals were stable and she'd actually managed to hold down a small breakfast this morning. The doctor had even mentioned releasing her later that afternoon. Relief washed over Beth as she said a silent prayer of thanks. It was so unfair that the girl might have to spend her final days so miserably. "Call me if anything changes, would you?"

Lucy agreed to call Beth if Laurie wasn't released that day. Beth knew how cautious her oncologist was. He no doubt felt extremely confident for the moment if he planned to send her home.

Beth hung up the receiver and turned around to

find Zach standing right behind her inside the granary office door. She couldn't quite stifle the gasp his unexpected presence elicited.

"Sorry. I didn't mean to startle you." That one-sided half grin that made her heart hurdle into an acrobatics routine slid into place.

"It's okay. I wanted to check on Laurie." Beth ignored her traitorous body's instant response to his.

"How's she doing?"

"Better." God, why did he have to look like he really cared beyond the usual basic human compassion? She didn't want to think about the kind way he'd been so patient last night, especially considering Mrs. Ellroy's strange behavior.

"Good." He hitched a thumb toward the warehouse area where the floats were coming together quite nicely. "Everyone else is heading out to lunch. Helen left with Viola. I told her you could catch a ride with me." He hesitated. "Unless you'd prefer to drive your own car."

He had reached the same conclusion as she had. She'd known it! Neither wanted to risk what they already had. Regret niggled at her. Now she would never know if Zach was everything she'd dreamed he was all these years. Though he certainly looked the part, she mused as her wicked side conjured up his naked image. Would she ever be able to put the "what if's" out of her head?

Beth smiled. "Or you could ride with me," she suggested.

He shrugged. "Whatever."

She cleared her throat and stepped past him. "Good. I'll drive." At least if she drove she'd be in control...to some extent anyway.

"About last night," he began, his words slowing her step.

Reluctantly she turned back to face him. "You don't have to say it," she said before he could. "It was a mistake. I know."

Beth didn't give him the opportunity to explain his reasoning with the fancy words that were the tool of his trade. She didn't want to discuss it. Not now. Not later.

She only wanted to forget that she had, yet again, behaved foolishly where Zach Ashton was concerned.

And just like fourteen years ago, she was still nothing but the girl next door as far as he was concerned.

As USUAL on a Saturday, the diner was jam-packed at half past noon. It was Kelso's only real restaurant in terms of a sit-down meal where a waitress served patrons at their tables, but in any other terms, restaurant only applied in the vaguest sense of the word. As a doctor, Beth recognized the possible hazards to one's health when choosing to nourish oneself at the diner. But that fact did little to discourage those seated around the tables at the moment.

Zach had ushered her to a booth near the back since almost every table was occupied. As she slid in on the opposite side from him, Beth waved at her mother who looked exasperated with Viola—which was typical. Viola would exasperate the Pope himself if given five minutes of his time. But she got things done for the city council. The woman was relentless when she championed a particular cause.

"Everything seems to be coming together," Zach

commented as he perused the worn menu. Yellowed and cracked vinyl covered the same handwritten items offered for as long as Beth could remember. She couldn't imagine why he even bothered to look.

Beth definitely didn't have to see a menu. She'd order her usual, a salad with dressing on the side. It was the safest item listed, if not the most palatable.

"Everyone likes the theme you selected."

"I'm glad." Glad wasn't really a strong enough description of what she felt—thrilled was the better word. She'd toyed with the friendship theme for days, but hadn't really fleshed it out. Now she was thankful she'd gone with her gut instinct. Swaying Viola and Mayor Chadwick from their queen-for-a-day theme wouldn't have been so easy had everyone else not latched on to the friendship concept and run with it.

"You did good." Zach gifted her with an approving smile.

Irritation stirred when her heart responded in its usual reaction. "I did leave out one thing," she began, the idea that had taken root days ago now blooming forth with renewed purpose. Why hadn't she remembered this before?

"What's that?" That analyzing blue gaze never deviated from hers as the waitress placed glasses of water before them.

"What can I get for you?"

Ignoring his question for the moment, Beth shifted her attention to the waitress. "A garden salad with vinaigrette on the side."

"And you?" the woman turned to Zach, her pen poised above her pad. The white uniform she wore appeared to be several sizes too small and shrink-wrapped on her slim body. Apparently, in an effort to make up for the lack of material in her uniform, she'd layered on the cosmetics.

"I'll take the blue plate special and a cola," he told her, punctuating his choice with a wide smile and just enough charm to send her oozing away.

"You like to live dangerously?" Beth inquired, annoyed that his display of charm made her feel a decidedly obvious stab of jealousy. No doubt women fell at his feet on a daily basis. He'd been right when he'd said he wasn't the marrying kind. Why hadn't she noticed that years ago? God, she was full of questions for herself today. Too bad she didn't have any answers.

Zach leaned back against the booth and draped his arms along the top of it. "From time to time," he replied, clearly amused by her current irritation. "Life can get rather boring if you don't teeter on the edge now and again."

"You should watch your cholesterol," she retorted, then sipped her water in an effort to cool the ire kindling inside her.

He chuckled. "Oh. You're talking about the food."

She refused to take the bait. "Yes. The *greasy* food."

"I think we've had that conversation before." The waitress returned with his cola. "Thanks, Wanda." His smile was full wattage this time. As irritated as she was, even Beth's pulse reacted.

"I had just one other suggestion for making your mother's birthday perfect," she said, drawing his attention back to her and away from the dramatically swaying hips of *Wanda* the waitress.

"What's that?" He glanced at Beth, then stared after the waitress a couple seconds more.

Fury erupted inside Beth. If she didn't know better she'd think he was purposely goading her. "The birthday serenade," she said pointedly.

Zach dragged his attention back to Beth with obvious reluctance. "Serenade?"

"Of course." Beth relaxed into the wide seat to enjoy watching him squirm. "You'll sing happy birthday to your mother. Solo. It'll be an unforgettable moment for her. I can see it now," Beth enthused.

Zach's expression fell instantly. "Me? A solo?" He made a disparaging sound in his throat. "I don't think so."

"Are you saying you can't do it?" she challenged. "Or you won't do it? This is a major milestone in your mother's life. Surely you're not going to let her down."

He leaned forward slightly. "That little guilt trip won't work, Beth, so don't even go there."

She shrugged. "I guess I'll just have to tell Mrs. Ashton that you don't want to do it."

"You mentioned it to her already?"

"Do you think I'd ask otherwise?" Beth hedged. It wasn't an out-and-out lie. She didn't actually say she'd told her...

He sighed, his own annoyance showing now. "Fine."

"Fine, you'll do it, or fine that I've told her and you don't care if it hurts her feelings?"

He glowered at her then. "Fine, I'll do it."

"Great. Your mother will cherish this birthday for the rest of her life."

Zach relaxed again, resigned to his fate. "So all that's left to do now is the rest of the decorating?"

Beth nodded. "Mayor Chadwick and his crew will finish the floats and organize the parade. Mother finally agreed this morning to oversee the caterers. All you and I have to do is decorate the west lawn and gazebo the day before."

"And pray it doesn't rain."

"Right."

"By the way," she said, feeling guilty herself for fibbing to him. "The gazebo looks terrific."

"Thanks."

He looked away again, as if her remark bothered him. Beth couldn't imagine why it would, but then the whole situation was awkward. Maybe last night had been a bigger mistake than even she knew at this point.

Silence fell between them. Beth tried to think of anything else related to the party that they needed to discuss, but nothing came. She focused on the veined marbling in the old Formica countertop to keep her gaze occupied. Where was their food? How long could it take to dish up a special and throw a few lettuce leaves in a bowl? Did he somehow think less of her after last night? Was his image of her tarnished now?

Her gaze bumped into Zach's and she couldn't be sure which of them looked away the fastest.

She had to know if the "they" they'd always been was still okay. There had to be something they could talk about.

"How are things in Chicago?" she said in a rush, then composed herself. "You know, with the Colby Agency."

"Great." Using one fingertip, he traced the path of a bead of condensation as it trickled down the side of his sweating water glass. "I miss it."

Another little prick of regret. "The work or the city?"

His gaze reconnected with hers. "Both."

Beth tried not to show her disappointment. This was just one of the many reasons that the other kind of "they" could never be. "Tell me about your work," she urged when she really wanted to know about his private life but wouldn't dare ask.

His private life.

In that instant Beth acknowledged just how little she knew about the man Zach had become. He'd left for law school fourteen years ago. She'd never forget that day...or that kiss. Though he'd come home many times for visits since, she'd pretty much avoided him. But the fact of the matter was she did actually know what kind of man he was. Not only had her mother bragged on him too many times to count, she also knew firsthand the way he'd been raised. The Ashtons were among the finest people she knew. Colleen in particular. To Beth's knowledge neither the woman nor her husband had ever done the first thing to harm anyone or anything.

"What would you like to know?" He took a drink from his cola and waited expectantly.

"Whatever you want to tell me, I suppose." Was he trying to make this conversation difficult? She just wanted to know what he did all day long. Really, she fumed, what is it a lawyer does? It wasn't like she was asking if he was still thinking about the waitress...or how many lady friends he had back in Chicago.

''I respond to legal inquires and make inquiries of my own,'' he said simply. ''Occasionally I argue a case in court, but not often. I can usually negotiate an understanding before it reaches that point.''

Oh, she would just bet he could negotiate anything he set his mind to. ''Does the Colby Agency find itself at the wrong end of a lawsuit often?'' That was Beth's next thought. As a doctor, lawsuits were a looming threat every single day.

''Not that often. We play by the rules and we're careful. Our investigators arc highly trained. They know what they're doing.'' He quirked one eyebrow, giving an even sexier appeal to his handsome face. ''That's not to say that they don't ever bend the rules. They just don't break them.''

Beth struggled to block thoughts of how good he looked. Now was not the time to let her guard down. She'd finally made up her mind once and for all and she couldn't let anything change it. Certainly not her carnal fantasies.

''Sounds interesting,'' she said, plastering a pleasant smile into place. ''Colleen tells Mom that Victoria Colby considers you the best there is in legal representation and that she'd be lost without you.''

A sheepish grin tugged the corners of his full lips into an unreasonably appealing tilt. ''Well, I try.''

Beth frowned a little as she remembered something else her mother had said. ''It sounds a little cloak-and-daggerish, if you know what I mean.''

''It's the nature of the beast,'' Zach explained. ''Sometimes it takes a smoke screen to see the clear picture.''

Worry sneaked its way into her heart. ''Are there times when your job is dangerous?''

He looked thoughtful for a moment, his attention seemingly back on the water glass. "In a business like the Colby Agency, you make a few enemies. Some are more powerful and vindictive than others. There's always the risk that someone will retaliate for an assumed wrong." He looked at her then, really looked at her. "I'm cautious, but I don't dwell on that aspect of my work. I love what I do. I can't imagine doing anything else anywhere else."

There it was. The heart of the matter. They were from two different worlds. She didn't belong in his any more than he did in hers. Why had she ever considered an affair with him? Didn't she know that she'd only end up with a broken heart...because he really would leave? The tiny fledgling sprout of hope that he might take her into his arms and ride off into the sunset to live happily ever after withered and died.

They would never be.

ZACH STARED out at the cottage from his bedroom window. They'd finished up at the warehouse hours ago. He'd stood in this window wishing he could tell Beth what he really wanted ever since. Darkness had long since fallen, but he'd see her pass the kitchen window from time to time. She'd gotten dressed up for some reason. Some sort of dress. He couldn't make out the details, but he didn't have to. He knew her sweet body by heart.

He closed his eyes for a moment and savored the memory of kissing her skin, of reveling in her body's response to him. She'd wanted him almost as badly as he'd wanted her. A smile nudged him when he thought about that belly button ring. Too sexy. He would never have guessed that little secret in a thousand years. He opened his eyes and continued watching for a glimpse of her.

She was right, though, last night had been a mistake. If he'd taken her, she would have been his in every way. He couldn't possibly have walked away without her then. Dragging her off to Chicago would have made her miserable. She'd have grown to resent him in the long run.

But no matter how his brain reasoned the whole thing out, he just couldn't, not deep down anyway, believe that it was a mistake. He told himself that she was right. He considered all the pros and cons and it was the only logical conclusion.

But a part of him, the part that had absolutely nothing to do with reason or logic, didn't accept that verdict.

He wanted her desperately. Loved her to distraction. Zach blew out a weary breath and braced his hands against the window frame. He had to stop thinking about Beth and anything physical. It wasn't happening. She'd realized her mistake, saving them both a lot of heartache.

It was a waste of time and energy to dwell on the issue any further. Zach knew when to admit defeat, though he rarely did so. This was different. This was Beth. He'd never have allowed things to go this far if she hadn't—

An unfamiliar car came to a stop in the drive. Zach peered down at it in an effort to note anything recognizable about the vehicle or the driver when he or she emerged.

It was a he.

Zach leaned closer to his window.

The man rounded his hood and headed for Beth's front door. He carried something in one arm... flowers.

Unbridled fury flamed inside Zach. What the hell was some guy, flowers in hand, doing at Beth's door? He was far too young to be there to see Helen. The door suddenly opened and Beth stood before the stranger. When the man leaned forward and kissed her cheek Zach saw red.

He was down the stairs and in the kitchen before he could see clearly again. He snagged up his excuse from the kitchen counter and strode out the back door and straight over to the cottage.

He glared at the guy's sedate-looking sedan. Gray in color, most likely a perfect match for the jerk's personality. He probably liked listening to Michael Bolton and watching sitcom reruns. And Beth, obviously. A new flash of fury swept through Zach. He pounded on the door and imagined that the weathered wood was the guy's face.

The door opened and Beth stared up at him. To say she looked surprised would have been a vast understatement. She looked downright befuddled.

"Oh, hello, Zach." She pulled the door closer to her side, blocking his view into the house. "What's up?"

Was that nervous tension he heard in her voice? He thrust the cup he held in her direction. "I need to borrow a cup of sugar," he said flatly.

She looked at the cup in his hand then at him, her expression confused. "What?"

"You heard me," he said, angling his head so that he could see beyond the half-closed door. "Sugar. I need a cup of sugar."

She accepted the cup. "Okay. Give me a minute and I'll get it for you."

She left him standing at the door which only made him that much angrier. He flattened one palm against it and shoved it inward. As he entered, Beth disappeared down the hall. Zach strolled on into the living room and surveyed it until he found what he was looking for.

The guy wasn't very tall, but not exactly short. He looked young and fit. When he turned around to see who'd entered the room he looked startled to find Zach. Zach instantly pegged him as a wimp.

Just like the guy she'd married before.

Zach crossed the room and stuck out his hand. "Zach Ashton."

The guy faltered just as Zach had known he would. "Lane..." He cleared his throat and accepted Zach's hand. "Lane Wiseman."

Zach applied just enough pressure to the handshake so Lane would understand who was boss. Lane? What kind of name was that for a guy? "You hail from around here, Lane?"

Lane tugged at his shirt collar. "Ah...no. I grew up in Bloomingdale, but I moved to Cartersville to join the hospital staff a couple of years ago. The administrator is my uncle."

Oh, gee, Zach mused. Uncle So-and-So had gotten him a job. This was great. Beth damn sure knew how to pick 'em. Another blast of unmanageable fury hit him.

"So you're a doctor?" Zach inquired, his tone rich with sarcasm.

"A radiologist to be precise," Lane replied, his face now flushed.

"You like being a radiologist?"

He nodded. "Sure. My uncle says I have a bright future ahead of me."

Zach lifted one eyebrow in question. Maybe the guy'd been overexposed. Radiology had to be a risky profession. Then again, maybe his bright future had nothing at all to do with his personality and skill or lack thereof.

"You married? Kids?" Zach pressed.

"Oh, no." Lane laughed and gestured lamely to the flowers lying on the sofa table. "No," he repeated.

Zach nodded. "You're here to see Beth," he suggested in a tone just shy of accusing.

The guy looked suddenly afraid...very afraid. "Well, yes...I mean...yes. She's very nice," he rambled on. "We work together."

Zach resisted the urge to roll his eyes and say duh. "Is this the first time you two have been out?"

Before the guy could answer, Beth walked in with the cup of sugar. Color had darkened her cheeks. She was furious. Zach almost smiled. Good.

"Here you go, Zach." She handed him the brimming cup. "Baking cookies again?"

He glowered at her. "Yeah." He shifted his gaze to Lane "Wimp" Wiseman. "Gingerbread men."

Lane swallowed hard.

"Have fun," Beth said cheerfully as she practically pushed Zach into the hall. "Lane and I are off to the movies."

Zach hesitated at the front door. "The movies?" Movie theaters were dark. He darted a lethal look at Lane, who hovered a few feet away. But then, Zach reasoned, it would be crowded on a Saturday night. Too many other people around for them to—

"Yes, the movies." Beth ushered him out, then smiled. "Remember the drive-in?" she asked sweetly.

Drive-in? The image of Beth in that gray sedan with Lane zoomed into vivid 3-D focus in Zach's brain. Zach remembered all too well what he'd done at the drive-in. He thought they'd closed that place down years ago.

"You mean that old place is still open?" he echoed his thought.

Although her smile remained intact, Zach could see the fury broiling in that dark gaze. "Pete Carson reopened it several years ago, when retro became the in thing. It's the most popular place in town."

Zach remembered Pete Carson, too. If he was running the joint there was no telling what kind of movies were shown there. The idea of Beth and Lane in a car with steamy windows...

Zach crushed that line of thinking. Beth was a good girl, she wouldn't—

"Have a nice night," she said by way of dismissal. "I know I intend to." She shut the door in Zach's face.

His mother's words about all the guys chasing Beth echoed in his brain, joining the image still churning there.

Zach pivoted and started back toward his house, the unneeded cup of sugar in his hand. Beth's personal life was none of his business. What the hell was he doing intruding like this?

Whatever she did was fine by him.

He wasn't her father or her husband. If she wanted

to date some loser who probably couldn't even get a job without his uncle's help, what did he care? It wouldn't be the first time she'd gone after the wrong guy.

She, apparently, had not learned from her mistakes.

But that wasn't his problem.

He was just the guy next door.

Chapter Ten

Beth reached into the bag for another fluffy kernel of salty popcorn and sighed, being careful that her *date* didn't hear her. She stole a stealthy sideways glance at Lane. He chose that precise moment to stuff a wad of popcorn into his mouth. She grimaced when the overflow fell into his lap as he began to chew what was clearly more than a mouthful. A couple of chews later and he washed it all down with a long, noisy draw from his cola.

Fixing her gaze back on the big screen, Beth reminded herself that he was the hospital administrator's nephew and a pretty nice guy, eating habits aside. She would never hurt his feelings, though she'd wished a million times she hadn't answered the telephone when he'd called. She frowned as she sipped her cola. In the four months that she'd been on staff at the hospital, he'd never asked her out before. She wondered at his sudden interest now. Maybe he was simply bored.

Saying no thanks hadn't really been an option, not only to spare his feelings but to protect her job as well. She saw on a daily basis how defensive the administrator was where his nephew was concerned.

Cartersville wasn't that much larger than Kelso, most everybody knew everyone else. The last thing she wanted to do was get on the administrator's wrong side.

Beth tried again to pick up the gist of the movie's plot, but she'd been lost in thought through most of it and it was half over now. She kept thinking about Zach showing up at her door asking to borrow a cup of sugar. Irritation flamed inside her even now at the thought. He'd been checking up on her. He wanted to know who was at her house and what they were doing. The very idea of him snooping like that!

Why? was the $64,000.00 question. He apparently had no interest in her other than as friends. And, she'd already admitted to herself that she didn't want to risk that friendship. But why did he have to lend credibility to her lustful thoughts of him by acting territorial where she was concerned?

The answer hit her right between the eyes. He didn't want her but he didn't want anyone else to have her either. It was a man thing. He'd seen another man in the area and he'd shown up to mark what he considered his personal territory.

Fury erupted inside her all over again. Matt had never acted that way. Not even that last year they'd lived together, as their relationship disintegrated. He'd been reserved and more than willing to give up on their marriage without a fuss.

Beth took another bite of popcorn to placate the state of depression settling over her as she considered her pathetic love life. She and Matt had seemed to have so much in common. Their work, their quiet nature. Staying home when they were off duty had been their favorite pastime. An occasional social function with their colleagues, or going out to dinner and a movie was all the excitement either of them had required. To a point. It didn't take Beth long to realize that something wasn't quite right—in the romance department. Excitement was lacking there as well.

As hard as she tried she couldn't stop comparing the differences between her husband and the man she'd loved her whole life. How could she have ever thought that the mutual respect and faint stir of attraction she and Matt felt for each other would be enough? Not when she'd had that one taste of wild, animal attraction the night she'd kissed Zach. Nothing or no one had ever made her feel that way again. Though she and Zach hadn't ever made love…the kiss had been proof positive that they could generate heat and excitement.

Warmth rushed through her veins as she recalled the vivid image of Zach completely naked stalking around his bedroom. Matt certainly didn't look anything like that. She'd seen her share of naked men in her profession, but she couldn't recall a single one who looked quite like Zach. And she'd certainly never been to bed with any of the other naked men she'd seen. Matt was the one and only.

Beth almost groaned. Zach was right. She was a good girl. She'd tried to make him believe there'd been other relationships, she'd even convinced herself that she could do an affair. But the truth was she hadn't once tried.

The bottom line was she had no real experience in the sex game and no one to compare anything to except Matt. And, well, Matt was Matt. He wasn't exactly stud material.

She stole another look at her date. Neither was
Lane for that matter. But he was a man. She looked
at him again, a little more closely this time. The light
from the movie flickered through the windshield,
highlighting his profile. He wasn't handsome like
Zach and he didn't have the same muscular body,
but he was nice. Unlike Zach's, Lane's lips were a
little on the thin side, and he didn't have much of a
chin. But he had a great sense of humor. And there
was no time like the present to start beefing up her
experience. She might even find that she liked Lane
enough to rid Zach from her system altogether.

What was she thinking? Beth felt suddenly ill. She
needed some fresh air…to splash her face with water.
Something. Anything to clear her head.

"I have to go to the rest room," she blurted. Her
stomach churned violently in emphasis of her statement. How could she have even thought about…?

She was losing her mind. She had to get out of
this car.

"Yeah, sure," Lane said without ever taking his
eyes off the screen. "I'll catch you up when you get
back so you don't miss anything."

Beth left her drink and popcorn on the console and
climbed out of the car, almost falling in her haste.
This was all Zach's fault. He was making her crazy.
She hurried through the rows of cars toward the refreshment center. Steamy windows concealed the
passengers of nearly every car she passed. Few had
bothered to place the speaker inside the window. She
frowned, her step slowing as she studied the cars on
either side of her. They couldn't hear the movie that
way. She doubted they could see either. Why would
they…?

Understanding dawned on her. Her mouth dropped open and she forced her feet back into motion. No wonder this place was so wildly popular. And all this time she'd thought it was the old movies they billed.

Surely Lane hadn't thought...? She shook her head. He was too busy actually watching the movie to want to...

What was wrong with her? Suddenly all she could think about was sex.

Just one more week, she told herself. In one more week Zach would be back in Chicago and her life could get back to normal. She'd store away all these silly notions and fantasies about him and never allow them to surface again.

All she had to do was survive this one week. Their friendship would be left unharmed and she would focus on her work just like before. She'd married once. Who said she had to do it again? Her work fulfilled her. She didn't need a husband or children. The vivid image of her belly, minus the belly button ring, ripe with Zach's child brought her to an abrupt stop. The sense of yearning that swamped her made her reach for the closest object to steady herself. She leaned against the trunk of someone's car and allowed the powerful sensation to fade.

Would she never know the feeling of holding her own child? Zach's child? Or of feeling his arms around her as she fell asleep at night? Would none of those things ever be? She'd dreamed of their being together somehow for so long, how would she ever live the rest of her life without touching that place in her heart again?

What if he married? A flood of pain cascaded over her. He'd never married before, but maybe he would in spite of his claims otherwise. Someone else would fall asleep in his arms, feeling loved and protected by the kind of man who knew how to make her feel both. That sick feeling welled in Beth's stomach again when she considered that it wouldn't be her.

The solid support beneath her suddenly started to rock. It took Beth a few seconds to figure out what was happening. When it finally hit her she shot to her feet.

Dammit. Was everyone here having sex but her?

Angry with herself for feeling so vulnerable and needy, she stormed the rest of the way to the refreshment center. She jerked the door open and went inside. The audio from the movie was piped in for those waiting in line. As if any of them cared. The part of the building that faced the movie screen was one long row of windows, tables flanked it for those who preferred to eat inside rather than in their cars. Retro fifties décor, including a car from the era, lent the proper ambiance to the newly refurbished building. A neon sign directed patrons to the rest rooms. Beth wove her way through the crowd, her frustration mounting with each male of the species she encountered.

Men! she fumed. Who needed them? They were confusing, self-centered creatures who did nothing but make the lives of women miserable. She should just swear off men altogether. In her experience, minimal as it was, sex was overrated anyway. So what if Zach could make her body burn. Just because a horse got out of the gate didn't mean it would win the race.

The next time she saw Zach Ashton she might just tell him to kiss her—

There he was. She froze halfway through the crowd.

What was he doing here?

His odd behavior earlier when he'd pretended to need a cup of sugar filtered through the haze of anger engulfing her brain. She remembered telling him where she and Lane were going. Zach was...

Her eyes widened as renewed fury swept through her. He was checking up on her.

Beth pushed her way through the crowd until she'd reached him. After tapping him on one broad shoulder, she demanded, "What the hell are you doing here?"

Pretending to be surprised at seeing her, he smiled that big old lopsided gesture that, as usual, made her heart react. "Hey, Beth. Enjoying the movie?"

"Don't try to change the subject," she snapped. "I asked what you're doing here?"

The teenager behind the counter interrupted, "What'll it be?" she asked Zach.

Zach, feigning confusion, turned to the kid and said, "Two large colas, two large popcorns." Then he turned back to Beth. "Is something wrong?"

She felt the blood drain from her face. Her anger reversed itself and instantly diverted to humiliation and utter jealousy. He'd ordered *two* colas and *two* popcorns. He wasn't checking up on her. He wasn't alone. He'd come to the drive-in with someone. A woman, no doubt. The blood that had forsaken her face now pooled in her feet, making it impossible for her to run, as she'd so like to.

"No," she squeaked. "Nothing's wrong. I...I just didn't expect to see you here."

Zach took out a bill and placed it on the counter

to pay for the items he'd ordered. "You didn't think I was checking up on you, did you?" he teased.

A new blast of anger sent color to her cheeks yet again and enough blood rushing back to her head to send her blood pressure into the red. "Don't be ridiculous. Why would I think such a thing?"

He shrugged one of those massive shoulders. "I don't know. Maybe it has something to do with you marching up to me and demanding to know what I'm doing here."

She lifted her chin and glared at him. "I'm an adult, Zach. Why would I care what you do?" Gritting her teeth to keep from saying more, she pushed between Zach and the guy behind him and all but ran down the hall to the rest room.

Once inside the small ladies' room, she sagged against the door and blew out a breath of pure frustration.

What was wrong with her?

She hadn't suffered with mood swings like this since junior high school. First she wanted to have an affair with the man, then she wanted nothing to do with him. Then she topped the whole thing off by humiliating herself right to his face.

He knew exactly what she'd thought.

He knew exactly how she felt.

She never could hide anything from Zach. With her mother's odd behavior, this out-of-control birthday celebration and Zach, Beth was ready to scream.

She clamped her mouth shut in case the urge overwhelmed her. If she screamed they'd lock her up and throw away the key. Especially considering her current behavior. No one in her right mind acted the way she'd been acting lately. She could just imagine

Lane telling his uncle all about her unstable behavior. Then she'd lose her job to boot.

A loud rap on the door jerked her back to the here and now. She placed a hand on her chest and drew in a steadying breath.

"Just a minute," she called out. A quick check in the mirror and a little cold water on her flushed face was all she needed. Surely whoever it was could wait that long. It was ridiculous that there wasn't more than one stall in an establishment this size. She supposed she should be thankful that it was so clean. She'd seen few public rest rooms this immaculate. She straightened away from the door.

"Beth, is everything all right?"

Zach.

Surprise, swiftly followed by fury, jolted her. She whipped around and glared at the wood panel that stood between her and the very man she wanted to escape.

"Would you please just go away," she demanded. A woman can't even go to the bathroom, she added silently.

"Why are you hiding from me?"

Her mouth fell open. She leaned closer to the door so there would be no mistaking her words when she spoke. "I am not hiding," she said succinctly. "Why would I?"

The nerve of him, she fumed. Hands planted on her hips, she dared him to argue the issue.

He didn't.

Instead, he opened the door and walked in, closing it behind him.

"What are you doing? You can't come in here!"

"What's going on, Beth?" That pulse-tripping

blue gaze leveled on hers. That muscular body blocked the only escape route, towering over her, making her want to lean into him and at the same time run like hell.

She backed up a step only to be halted by the one stall in the tiny room. "If someone else comes in and finds you in here like this, Zach Ashton, I swear I'm going to—"

He reached behind him and locked the door. "No one's coming in."

Something in his eyes, a kind of heat and determination she'd never seen before, sent her heart hammering into overdrive. "You can see that I'm fine," she told him, trying her best to keep the tremor from her voice. "Now, would you please leave."

He stepped forward. Her eyes widened.

"Not until you admit," he said silkily, "that you thought I was checking up on you."

"I thought no such thing," she denied. This time she couldn't tell if her voice wavered or not, the blood roaring in her ears muffled all other sound. Heat followed its path, making her too warm inside the thin cotton dress. Making her want to squirm beneath his penetrating gaze.

"Liar," he murmured.

He was way too close. She couldn't think with him this close. "You can't be certain that I'm not telling the truth."

"And you can't be sure I don't have a lady waiting in the car for me."

Her gaze zeroed in on his lips as he spoke, but his words jerked her attention back to his eyes. "Then I'd suggest that you don't keep her waiting any longer." It was probably Wanda the waitress, Beth seethed. She remembered the way the woman had flirted with Zach and how he'd poured on the charm.

"We have to talk first," he returned as if he had all night and not another care in the world.

Beth presented a caustic smile. "Talk to the wall, Zach, because I'm not listening." Before he could cut her off she'd slipped into the stall and slid the tiny lock into place.

"I'm not playing games with you, Beth. Now come out here so we can talk."

"When hell freezes over," she retorted sweetly. She closed the lid on the toilet seat and sat down. She wasn't going anywhere until she was good and ready and that wouldn't be until he'd left the ladies' room. She crossed one leg over the other and smoothed a hand over the hem of her dress. Surely Lane would come looking for her eventually and then Zach would have to leave.

Zach glowered at the locked stall door before him. He wasn't going anywhere until they settled this once and for all. So what if he was checking up on her. It was a funny thing to him that he'd been in town all week and she'd hadn't once gone out on a date or even mentioned a boyfriend and suddenly she's out with Wiseman. Zach knew exactly what she was up to. She was trying to make him jealous. If Wiseman was really her boyfriend, she wouldn't have been on the verge of making love with Zach just the other night.

His groin tightened to the point of pain at the memory of touching her as he'd dreamed of doing for so long. He clenched his jaw and reminded himself that he wasn't supposed to be thinking that way anymore. He was supposed to be protecting Beth.

And that was exactly what he intended to do. She sure as hell didn't need a guy like Wiseman. If she couldn't see that then he'd just have to show her.

He might as well start by telling her what a mistake she was making. What kind of friend would he be if he looked the other way? "I hope you're not serious about this guy," he said bluntly.

Silence.

"Think about it," Zach went on when she didn't respond. "He might be the hospital administrator's nephew, which could, I suppose, be good for you career-wise, but do you really want to spend the rest of your life with a guy named Lane?" Zach shook his head at the thought. "Personally, I think it would be another huge mistake."

The stall door opened.

Beth glared at him with a mixture of fury and disbelief. "You're giving me advice on my love life when you've never even been involved in a long-term relationship?"

The same outrage he heard in her voice lit inside him. "Who says I've never been in a long-term relationship?"

She hitched a thumb at her chest. "I do. You're too busy with your career to take time to do anything more than charm them into the sack."

"Charm them into the sack?" Absolute fury mushroomed inside him. "If you're talking about the other night, I seem to recall you asked me to take you to bed."

She poked him in the chest with her index finger. "You didn't appear to have a problem with it," she snapped right back.

He leaned slightly closer, going for intimidation.

"I didn't have a problem. I just don't like being used."

"Used? I'm not even going to try to figure that one out. Maybe you stayed in the sun too long or inhaled too many paint fumes the other day when you were working on the gazebo. Because I can tell you right now that you're definitely not thinking straight."

"Why'd you need me if you had Lane?"

She blinked. Uncertainty flashed in her eyes. Dammit. He hadn't meant for it to come out that way. Now she would know.

"You think I wanted to have an affair with you because things weren't working out between Lane and me?" Her tone sounded every bit as incredulous as the expression on her face looked.

Zach swore silently. "What do you expect me to think?"

The uncertainty in her eyes turned to amusement. "You think Lane can't…so I…" Laughter overtook her ability to speak.

Fury whipped through Zach all over again. There wasn't a damned thing funny about any of this. "It isn't that funny," he growled when she continued laughing.

She wiped her eyes and pressed her fingers to her lips to try and hold back her mirth. "I'm sorry," she finally blurted. "I just can't stop laughing."

Zach silenced her with his mouth. The taste of her sweet lips beneath his undid him completely. His arms went around her waist and pulled her against him. He wanted to feel the heat of her soft body. He wanted to touch all of her…to kiss her until neither of them could think straight. Her arms wound around his neck and she returned his kiss with abandon. Her tongue darted into his mouth tempting him beyond all reason.

A cloak of heat and desire enveloped them, co-cooning them in pure sensations. His hands trailed down her back and molded to her shapely buttocks. He lifted her against his hips, his body already rigid with need. She moaned softly, sending his protective instincts soaring. He wanted to know her completely. He worked his fingers beneath the hem of her short dress and lifted her hips against his once more. She wrapped those lush thighs around his waist and time and place deserted him. She undid button after button, then spread open his shirt so that she could touch him. He groaned his approval, the feel of her fingers searing his chest.

Still devouring her mouth, he pressed her against the wall and ground the part of him that ached so fiercely into her feminine heat. She cried out, the sound lost to their kiss. Her hands found their way to the waist of his jeans and she struggled to unfasten them.

"Wait," he murmured against her lips.

"Can't," she whispered back, her fingers still tugging.

Helpless to do otherwise, he held her in place with one hand and wrenched his jeans open with the other. She eased one small hand inside, her soft, warm fingers molding around him. He groaned. She caressed the length of him and he shuddered with anticipation.

"Hurry," she breathed.

He nodded, his mouth hovering only centimeters above hers. He pulled aside the silky panel of her panties and sank into the tight, wet, heat of her. He didn't stop until he was buried completely inside her. The sensation was so powerful he couldn't move for one long moment, he could only savor the feel of mating with Beth.

Her fingers dug into his shoulders.

He moved, just once. She cried out, the sound echoing around them. His body jerked in response to the unbearably sweet tightening of hers.

"More," she demanded, bracing her feet against the opposite wall to give her purchase. She arched against him, urging him into action.

Things were moving too fast for him to maintain control. She arched again.

She pulled his head back down to hers. "More," she murmured again then crushed her mouth onto his.

He obeyed, helpless to do otherwise. He thrust deeply, drew back, then thrust again. Every part of him was focused on pleasing her...touching her... tasting her. Learning this part of Beth he'd never known before. She climaxed, the throbbing, contracting of her feminine muscles drawing on the release he wanted to hold back just a little while longer. She kissed him harder, sucked on his tongue, forcing him over the edge. His movements quickened, shallow at first, then so deeply that she screamed his name. He surrendered, coming hard and fast.

He pressed his forehead to hers and commanded his body to stop trembling. He'd never lost it like this before. Their ragged breathing was the only sound in the room. "Beth, I—"

"Don't say anything."

He could already feel her body tensing in his arms

as the reality of their frantic act filtered through the lingering aftermath. He wanted to kick himself. He'd just made love to Beth. Instead of making the moment special, he'd taken her like...like this, not even taking time to protect her from any possible consequences of their impulsiveness. He swore softly. How would he ever make this up to her?

"I have to get out of here." She scrambled out of his arms and pushed him away.

She slipped out of the stall before he'd pulled himself together.

"Beth, wait."

She rushed away without looking back.

He slammed a fist into the wall. What the hell had he been thinking following her in here like this? He swore again as he jerked the door open and started out.

A feminine shriek brought him up short.

The woman had apparently started into the bathroom when he opened the door. "Excuse me," he muttered. The woman flattened against the wall, giving him ample room to pass and only stared, wide-eyed, at him.

Too consumed with Beth to take the time to placate the woman further, he rushed through the crowd still lined up around the counter, searching every face for Beth's. She'd gone back to Wiseman's car already. Ire twisted in Zach's gut at the thought. He hurried outside and double-timed it to where the guy had parked. Zach only got a glimpse of his taillights as Wiseman drove away.

Zach blew out a weary breath.

He'd royally screwed up this time. Though his body still hummed with the pleasure of having Beth, his brain knew he'd done it all wrong. And she, most likely, would never forgive him. Not that he'd blame her.

Disgusted with himself, Zach made his way back to his car. He opened the driver's side door and dropped behind the wheel.

"Where's my popcorn and soda?"

He smacked himself on the forehead with the heel of his hand and swore yet again.

"You've been gone all this time and you didn't get what you went after," his mother demanded. "Heavens to Betsy, son, where's your head?"

If she only knew.

He opened the car door and looked at his mother before getting out. "Sorry. I'll get it now."

She stared at him, her face registering disapproval. "Well, before you do, take a moment to pull yourself together, would you?"

She looked him up and down, noting the button he'd missed on his shirt and the hasty manner in which he'd tucked it into his jeans. Details he'd failed to notice before.

"My God, son, you look like you've just had sex."

Chapter Eleven

Beth paced the living room Sunday morning. Her mother had gone to early mass and to do her usual Sunday visits. Unable to risk her mother's too perceptive eyes, Beth had remained in her room until she was sure she was gone. Now she had only her own self-deprecating thoughts with which to contend.

How could she have allowed things to get so out of control last night? She should never have approached Zach in the first place. The idea that Lane had waited, unknowing, in the car for her just as Zach's unknown lady friend—Beth clenched her jaw—had waited for him made Beth feel ill. She'd never done anything so underhanded in her life. What was worse, she'd run back to Lane's car, Zach's essence still clinging to her skin, and demanded that Lane take her home. The man surely thought she was one card shy of a full deck.

She had to be! She'd had sex with Zach in the ladies' room at the drive-in. She flung her arms out in exasperation and plopped down on the sofa. She dropped her face into her hands and groaned. How could she have allowed this to happen?

How would she ever face Zach again?

He'd…everything inside her stilled as she replayed last night's desperate act. The memory of the way he'd kissed her sent butterflies into flight in her stomach. He kissed her as if she were the one and only woman on Earth he wanted. She could feel the longing in him…could taste his yearning. He'd been as desperate as she had been. He hadn't wanted it to be that way, she knew. He'd hesitated, but she'd urged him on and he'd complied. Her heart swelled to near bursting as her mind relived the pleasure of his touch…his possession.

She couldn't find the proper words to describe how he made her feel—desperate, out of control, yet complete. That was it. Beth rose from the sofa. He made her feel complete. A kind of calm settled over her with the realization. Her entire adult life the only time she felt that way was when he was near. No matter how she tried to deny it, it was true. She prayed that somehow she made him feel that way, too. But she couldn't be sure. How much of his feelings were protective versus amorous? Just because he wanted her happy and safe didn't mean he loved her the way she loved him.

Beth sighed mightily. Why was she berating herself about this? The whole issue was moot. Zach was leaving in just one week. The day after his mother's party. Beth froze. Next Saturday was Colleen's birthday which made yesterday…she did the math.

"Oh, God."

They hadn't…

"Oh, God," she repeated, collapsing onto the sofa once more.

This was the very worst time of the month that

she could have had unprotected sex. Her cycles were as regular as clockwork. Beth felt suddenly cold and just a little afraid. Though she trusted Zach implicitly not to risk her safety in any way...neither of them had stopped to consider the other consequences of what they were doing.

She could be pregnant.

Beth reminded herself to breathe. She inhaled, exhaled, then lost her breath all over again at the thought of having Zach's child.

But he wouldn't want this. He'd already told her that he wasn't the marrying kind...he was too busy for a wife and a family. A new wave of fear swept over her. She had her mother. She wouldn't be alone if...

She stood and started pacing again. She was worrying for nothing. As a doctor she knew that there was just as good a chance that if she were ovulating, which she probably was, that she wouldn't conceive as there was that she would. It was ridiculous to worry about it anyway. She'd drop by the lab next week and have her friend Cindy run a blood test just to put her mind at ease. For the moment she would simply put it out of her mind. No point in borrowing trouble.

A soft rap on the front door startled her. Surely no one from the town council would stop by on a Sunday morning to discuss Colleen's celebration. Beth frowned. She did recall Colleen mentioning that she wanted to talk to her. The woman was every bit as perceptive as Beth's own mother. She'd have to watch her p's and q's. Taking a moment to catch her breath before she opened the door, Beth reminded herself that she was probably worrying for nothing.

Everything would be fine. She most likely was not pregnant and a frantic quickie with Zach didn't constitute a lifetime commitment. There was no reason, she told herself once more, to borrow trouble.

Beth opened her front door and looked up into Zach's handsome face.

Nope. She didn't need to borrow trouble, it was at her door. Her heart kicked into warp speed the moment their gazes locked.

He opened his mouth to speak, but closed it when no words were forthcoming. He ran a hand through his hair and over his neck and peered down at her with such pain and regret that she felt moved to reach out to him.

"Has something happened?" Her fingers tightened around his arm and she pulled him inside. "Is your mother all right?"

"She's fine," he finally said, his gaze still so solemn that it made Beth's chest ache.

In spite of all her anxiety, she couldn't deny how good he looked and the fact that she noticed. She let go of his arm for fear of clinging foolishly or rushing into those strong arms. The dark gray trousers lent elegance while the matching polo shirt molded to his muscular torso in a way that spelled danger. To her heart anyway.

He exhaled a big breath and flared his hands, his beautiful blue eyes searching hers. "I'm sorry, Beth." He looked away a moment. "I didn't want it to be that way, but things went a little crazy and..." His voice trailed off.

He was apologizing for last night. Beth's heart sank. He hadn't meant for it to happen...he hadn't really wanted to make love with her. She'd been the one forcing the issue all along. Now he was sorry.

She summoned her bravest tone. "There's no need to apologize. If anyone is to blame, it's me. I started this whole thing. As you said before, yours was simply a typical male reaction."

He didn't look at her for a long moment, when he finally did, something had changed in his eyes. The regret looked a lot more like impatience. The pain had vanished. "Is that what you think?"

She didn't know what she thought, but if she wasn't confused before she was now. "What should I think?"

The determination and heat she remembered from last night was suddenly back, only stronger. "That we made love and it wasn't how I wanted our first time together to be."

Their *first* time? Beth told herself to take a breath. "And how did you want it to be?" she asked, her voice small and uncertain.

He moved closer to her, but didn't touch her. She could feel his need to do just that, but he held back. She watched the battle taking place in his eyes, desire and denial. He wanted her again. And, dammit, she wanted him. But both feared the consequences.

"I wanted it to be special…like you," he said softly. "A moment you'd never forget. I wanted it to be worth the risk."

"The risk?" Could he know her other concern already?

"Of where we go from here." He did touch her then, the gentlest caress along her cheek. "I know you've worried about that, too."

Relieved nearly beyond words, she offered him a smile. "I have. So what do we do?"

His gaze turned solemn again. "I don't want to hurt you, Beth."

She firmed her courage. She was tired of being protected. "I'm well aware of when you're leaving if that's what concerns you." She was a grown woman. She'd wanted this affair and now it had begun, in a manner of speaking. Why not enjoy it to the fullest? She would know the consequences soon enough...and she would pay the price.

For the first time in her life, Beth understood what she really wanted. She wanted whatever she and Zach could have right now. She didn't want to think about tomorrow or next week or next year. She wanted to enjoy him...the way she'd dreamed of doing for so very long. She was an adult, she could handle the side effects.

Whatever they might prove to be.

"I'm not sure I can go back and just pretend that it...we didn't happen." He stared at the floor for a time, then continued, "You're not like other women. You're..."

"All grown up, Zach. I'm fully capable of facing the consequences of my actions."

He sighed. "Point taken." That slow, half grin tilted his mouth. "There is that one outstanding issue."

She moistened her lips in anticipation. "And what issue is that?"

He edged closer still. "I'd like the opportunity to rebut last night's performance." He teased that sensitive place near her ear with his lips. "If it pleases the court," he murmured.

Beth's every objection melted as those wicked lips made a path down her throat. "I think we need to discuss this in my chambers," she suggested, her words punctuated with a low moan of pleasure. "There's just one thing I have to know first."

"Anything." He kissed her lips, lingering until she almost lost her mind.

"Admit you were checking up on me last night," she demanded between his mind-blowing kisses.

He smiled against her lips. "Guilty."

She stilled, drawing back slightly. "And the lady waiting in your car?"

That smile eased into a wicked grin. "My mother."

Laughter bubbled up in Beth's throat, but just like last night, Zach quickly silenced her. He scooped her into his arms and carried her to her room. They undressed each other slowly, taking the time to savor each moment. His kisses made her tremble. His sure, masterful hands moved over her body like those of a magician gifted in the art of pleasure. His ministrations were so slow, so thorough that Beth felt ready to fall over the edge of control well before the first nudge of his possession. When he sank into her she knew without a doubt that she was whole again. She almost wept with the sweetness of it.

She grabbed his waist and pulled him hard against her, urging him to send her into that place of pure sensation.

"Easy, baby," he murmured against her skin. "I'm going to do this right this time."

LATER BETH lay in his arms, knowing that she would never be the same again. No man would ever make her feel this way. She knew that for a certainty now. He'd brought her pleasure over and over before taking his own. His lovemaking ability took her breath, even now, just thinking about the way he'd made her feel.

The telephone on her bedside table rang.

"Don't answer it," he said, his arms tightening around her.

"Have to," she murmured. She dragged the receiver to her ear and managed a hello.

"Dr. Elizabeth McCormick?"

"Yes." She pulled free of Zach's hold and sat up on the edge of the bed. "This is Dr. Dan—McCormick."

"Dr. McCormick, this is Ferris Wayland from Sacred Heart Hospital in Chicago. I apologize for calling on Sunday."

The rest of the conversation was too startling for Beth to fully comprehend everything the man said, but the bottom line was he'd called to offer her a position at his private facility. Apparently one of her med school professors had recommended her for the position. Dr. Wayland suggested a salary that was almost double her current one. She promised to let him know within the next week and hung up the phone, still reeling with aftershock.

"What was that all about?" Zach asked.

He'd joined her on the side of the bed. She smiled as her eyes gloried in admiring his completely naked and stunningly perfect masculine physique.

"That," she told him in all sincerity, "was strange. An administrator from a private hospital in Chicago calling to ask if I'd be interested in a position there."

Zach's instincts went on instant alert. "I thought you were happy here." She'd almost said Daniels...Dr. Daniels. Why the hell was she still using *his* name?

Beth shrugged. "I am. It's the strangest thing. I haven't applied for any positions elsewhere. He insists that one of my old professors recommended me for the position."

Zach refused to acknowledge the hope taking shape in his chest. If Beth took a position in Chicago... This wasn't right somehow. Though he certainly believed in God, he didn't quite believe in these kinds of coincidences.

"Are you going to seriously consider it?" He purposely kept the emotion out of his tone.

She looked at him, her gaze narrowing. "Why wouldn't I?"

He shrugged. "I don't know. I thought you didn't like city life."

With an impatient huff she snatched up her dress and stepped into it, giving him a great view as she wiggled into the sheath. But the topic under discussion was too serious for him to smile.

"Is there a law against changing my mind?"

He couldn't speak for a moment since his full attention was focused on watching her drag her panties up those long, shapely legs and over that gorgeous bottom.

"No...of course not," he managed to say. "It's just that it seems a little sudden."

She glowered at him then. Obviously he wasn't making himself clear. He stood and reached for her. She dodged his touch. He frowned.

"Don't worry, Zach. I'm not trying to follow you

back to Chicago. If I decide to take this position, it won't have anything to do with you or our..." She glanced at the rumpled sheets of her bed. "...*affair*."

Ire sprouted. *Affair?* What was wrong with him? Of course it was just an affair. Just because this was Beth and he thought he'd felt the earth move didn't mean a damned thing...obviously.

"I didn't think it would," he snapped, then grabbed up his trousers. He hesitated. "Why do you still use Daniels?"

"What?"

"Your ex's name. Why do you still use it?"

She glanced at him. "Because when I first moved here the divorce wasn't final. Afterward, I didn't want to confuse my patients."

That sounded reasonable, he supposed.

"Beth! I'm home."

Both of them froze at the sound of Helen's voice as she singsonged her greeting. The front door slammed and Beth jerked back into action.

"You have to get out of here," she whispered sharply, thrusting his shirt at him.

"How am I supposed to do that?" he demanded as he stepped into his loafers, took the shirt and at the same time grabbed his scattered socks. He wanted to shake her. Not only did he have the distinct feeling that she wasn't telling him the whole truth where this out-of-the-blue job offer was concerned, she wanted to hide their *affair* from her mother.

She sure knew how to deflate a guy's ego.

"Here," she ordered, still whispering. She pointed to the window.

Zach swore silently as he stomped over to the window and raised the lower sash. Lucky for him the cottage was only one story. He had one leg out and was about to duck through the window when Beth stopped him.

He glanced at the hand on his shoulder then at her. As angry as he was, her sweet smile made his heart lurch.

"Thank you. This morning was very special. I'll always remember it."

He couldn't help himself. He grabbed her with his free hand and kissed her with all the emotions churning inside him. Emotions he didn't fully understand. She cupped his face with her soft hands and kissed him back.

"Beth! Are you in there?" Helen called through the closed door.

Zach reluctantly released her. "Later," he promised, then slipped away. He heard the window close behind him but he didn't look back. If he looked back now, he wouldn't be able to leave. No matter what Helen or anyone else thought, he would have walked back up to that window, climbed back inside and kissed Beth again.

Because whether she knew it or not, she was his.

In every sense of the word.

"WE HAVE TO TALK."

At the sound of Helen's voice Colleen looked up from her novel, the long-awaited sequel to her all-time favorite. The tone and the look on her old friend's face told her this wasn't going to be pleasant. Not to mention it meant she wouldn't be getting back to her book for some time.

Colleen sighed and carefully marked the page before setting her new favorite book aside on the cocktail table. "Well, sit down and tell me what's put a bee in your bonnet now."

Helen sat down on the club chair directly across from her. She looked weary enough that Colleen's attention perked up. This must really be serious, she decided.

"They're having a...relationship," Helen said tightly.

Colleen suppressed the urge to jump up and do a little jig. Instead, she angled her head and looked directly at her friend with all the skepticism she could muster. "Really, and why would you think that?"

Helen glared at her. "Unless my daughter has taken to wearing men's silk boxers, I'd say that's the case."

One eyebrow inched a tad higher than the other. "You found a pair of silk boxers in your house?"

"In Beth's room under the edge of the bed."

Colleen tapped her chin thoughtfully. "What about that young man she had a date with? Lane or Blaine or whatever?"

Helen's glare grew more pointed. "That's another thing we need to discuss."

Colleen feigned indignation. "Why would you want to discuss your daughter's social life with me?"

"Because I know you set that up. Beth hasn't dated anyone since her divorce. She told me herself that she wasn't interested right now."

"I might have mentioned her stagnant social life to Lawrence the last time we talked." Colleen smoothed an imaginary wrinkle from her skirt. "I can't remember for a certainty, mind you."

"You always have had a selective memory."

Colleen lifted her chin and gave her friend a challenging look. "You're just mad because you didn't think of it first."

"I didn't think of calling Chicago first either," Helen accused.

"Chicago?" Colleen assumed a put-upon expression. "Why I haven't a clue what you're proposing."

"I'm proposing," Helen said hotly, "that you're paving the way for my daughter to follow your son back to Chicago."

Colleen shucked all pretenses then. "Would that be such a bad thing?"

"Of course not. Not if it's what they both want."

"I believe that may very well be the case. I've seen the way Zach looks at Beth. He's in love with her. Anyone can see that."

"I'm not blind, Colleen," Helen relented. "I know how the two of them feel, probably better than they do. But they don't know the whole story. That could change things."

Colleen tensed. "I've told you I won't discuss that subject with you. We've agreed to disagree."

"Risk your relationship with your son, if you please," Helen warned. "But I will not risk the one I have with my daughter."

"Don't forget your promise, Helen McCormick," Colleen cautioned. "Because I certainly won't."

Helen stood. She looked at Colleen for two beats then left without even saying goodbye. Colleen let go a shaky breath. Time was running out for her. Though she trusted Helen completely, she wasn't sure how much longer she could fight the battle that had been more than three decades in coming.

BETH PICKED AT her dinner that evening. Her mother had made a wonderful pot roast, just the way Beth liked it. But her appetite had vanished hours ago as she pondered her predicament. She kept replaying that kiss Zach had stolen before disappearing out her bedroom window. The promise of "later" he'd made. She trembled inside at the mere thought of being with him again.

Then there was that job offer. If she were in Chicago, maybe there was a chance things could work out between the two of them. She stabbed at a lettuce leaf and scolded herself. That was ridiculous. Zach had already told her that he wasn't interested in marriage. What if she relocated to be near him only to lose him when he grew bored with her? What would she do then?

"Not hungry, dear?" her mother suggested, interrupting Beth's worrisome musings.

She summoned a smile. "I'm just thinking about that call from Mr. Wayland."

Helen stared at her plate. It wasn't until then that Beth noticed that her mother had hardly touched her dinner as well.

"Is something bothering you, Mom?"

"No. I'm fine." She moved the food around on her plate, not choosing to eat any of it. Not even the potatoes, which were her personal favorite.

"It looks like your appetite is missing, too."

Helen looked up, tears glittering in her eyes.

Worry crept into Beth's heart. "Mom, you and Colleen aren't fighting again, are you?"

"Excuse me." Helen pushed back her chair and hurried from the room.

Startled and confused, Beth followed her. She

found her mother staring at the collage of family photographs on the mantel in the living room.

Beth came up behind her and stood silently for a long moment. "Don't push me out. Let me help."

Helen shook her head. "You can't help. This isn't a medical problem."

"I can at least listen," Beth insisted, disappointed that her mother would assume if it wasn't a medical problem she couldn't help.

"I know about you and Zach."

Beth took a moment to absorb the impact of her words. "I see."

Helen faced her, a somber combination of emotions wrenching her features. "No, you don't see."

The worry Beth had felt only moments ago was now replaced by fear. "What is it I don't see? What are you keeping from me?"

Helen wiped her eyes with her hands, no longer able to hold the tears at bay. She leveled her gaze on Beth and shook her head. "You don't know how much it pains me to tell you this, but I can't keep this secret any longer." She swayed with the weight of whatever was making her cry.

Beth took her mother by the arms and steadied her. "This secret, is it what you and Colleen have been at odds about?"

Helen nodded. "She doesn't want to let the truth come out, but I can't risk you being hurt with what she and I did all those years ago."

"Let's sit down." Beth guided her mother to the sofa and sat down next to her. She had a feeling that staying vertical wasn't going to be easy for either of them if what Helen was about to say was half as bad as it sounded.

She waited for Helen to regain her composure a bit, then she said. "Now, tell me what this is all about."

Helen looked directly at her, her eyes weary. "First, you have to promise me that you will never repeat what I'm about to tell you unless it's a matter of life and death."

Beth frowned. "All right. I won't say a word to anyone."

"Think, Beth," Helen cautioned. "When you say anyone that includes Zach, too."

Beth thought about that for a moment, then she nodded. "I understand. I won't betray your confidence."

Helen smiled faintly. "I know you won't."

"So." Beth took a deep, steadying breath. "Tell me."

"Before you and Zach were born, Colleen and I both had tried for many years to conceive."

Beth resisted the urge to press her hand to her abdomen as she listened to her mother's words.

"Your father and I weren't too worried because I was only twenty-seven and there was still plenty of time before fearing that it might not happen at all. We were both healthy and there was just no reason to be concerned."

Beth nodded, urging her mother to continue when she fell silent for a moment or two.

"But that wasn't the case with Colleen. She was thirty-seven and she'd just found out that there was a problem."

"A problem?" Beth studied her mother's face for any sign of what came next, but couldn't quite decipher the tangle of emotions she saw there.

"Colleen sought out a specialist in Chicago. He discovered that for some reason, which they didn't understand at the time, Colleen's body created antibodies to her husband's sperm. Because of that she would never be able to conceive."

Beth laughed, a short choked sound. "But that's ridiculous. She had Zach."

Helen's lips trembled and tears welled in her eyes once more. "No," she said tautly. "She didn't."

Numbness settled over Beth. "What do you mean she didn't?"

"Understandably Colleen was devastated by the news." Helen shook her head. "She didn't tell a soul except me. Well, and her husband. He knew, of course."

"This can't be," Beth denied.

Helen smiled and squeezed Beth's hand. "You see, I loved Colleen very much. Still do. She's like a sister to me. I would have done anything in the world to have helped her." She moistened her lips and took a deep breath. "So, I did. By complete accident I came upon this young girl who lived outside Indianapolis. She was visiting some of her folks in Cartersville." Helen frowned, concentrating. "She was barely eighteen. She was pregnant and unmarried." Helen shrugged. "She was desperate. And so was Colleen."

Beth swallowed. She knew what was coming. Oh, God, this couldn't be.

"Colleen made her an offer she couldn't refuse. The girl would get a fresh start, the money to go to college, her own home, whatever she needed. And Colleen would get the child."

Beth shook her head. This just couldn't be.

Helen squeezed her hand tighter. "To keep anyone from knowing that the child wasn't actually hers, Colleen went to Chicago. Zacharius told everyone that she was caring for an elderly aunt and wouldn't be back for months. The girl joined Colleen there and they stayed until the child was born."

"But how...I mean, what did they tell everyone when Colleen returned with a baby?"

"They simply explained that because they'd waited so very long to have a child and any number of things could have gone wrong that they'd chosen not to tell anyone until the child was safely in this world."

"What about a birth certificate?"

"The young woman pretended to be Colleen when she gave birth at the clinic in Chicago. No questions were asked."

Beth rubbed her forehead. This was crazy. She couldn't believe Colleen would *buy* a baby. Dear God. Zach. How would he take this?

"I can't believe Colleen would do anything like this," Beth insisted. It was like something from a movie. Things like this didn't happen to real people, especially not upstanding people like the Ashtons.

"Before you go judging her too harshly," Helen warned, "think long and hard about how desperately she wanted a child. How much she loves Zach. She and Zacharius gave him anything he ever wanted. Would you rather he have been an illegitimate child born to a mother without a high school education and with no way to support herself much less a child?"

"No." Beth shook her head. She was confused. "It's just such a shock. Keeping this from Zach all this time..."

"And you must do the same thing. You can't say a word."

Reality crashed down on Beth then. She'd promised she wouldn't tell anyone.

"The only reason I'm telling you this is to protect you. I can't just sit back and let you go falling in love with the man without knowing all the facts. I love you too much to let that happen."

Beth wasn't surprised that her mother saw through her so easily. As usual her mother was right. Beth was definitely head over heels in love with Zach. And she knew all too well how this secret, if he ever discovered the truth, would devastate him.

He was adopted…no…bought and paid for.

If he ever found out she'd kept this from him…

"What are we going to do?"

Her mother shook her head. "There's nothing we can do. It's out of our hands."

Chapter Twelve

Saturday had arrived. The parade was only a few hours away when Zach, with Beth's help, hung the last of the streamers and ribbons on the gazebo. He stood back then and admired his handiwork.

"Not bad, Ashton," Beth said. "Although I do think the one on the left is a little lower than the one on the right."

He climbed down from the ladder, grabbed her and kissed her soundly on the mouth. "I'm tired of working." He nipped her lower lip. "I want to play."

Beth shooed him away. "Stop it. You're going to shock our mothers."

He draped one arm around her shoulders and pulled her close while they both admired the decorating they'd done. "I think my mother is unshockable."

"Really." Beth looked up at him. "What makes you think that?"

Zach grinned. "Oh, just a feeling I have." He hadn't forgotten the wicked amusement in his mother's eyes that night at the drive-in. She was quite pleased that he and Beth were "involved" as she labeled it.

The grin left Zach's lips. Involved wasn't exactly the right word for what he felt. He wasn't even sure he could leave tomorrow. As much as he loved his work, the thought of leaving Beth behind was more than he could tolerate. So he didn't think about it. Apparently, she was avoiding thoughts of the future as well. He'd asked her at least three times what she'd decided about the job offer and she'd played the whole thing off. He had a bad feeling that she wasn't as ready to go back to city life as she'd insinuated.

"We did good," she said, then looked up at him. She frowned at what she saw before he could mask his feelings. "Why the long face?"

He kissed her nose. "I'm just thinking that it's going to be late this evening before we can get together."

"It won't be that late." She curled her arms around his waist, taking his breath. "I was thinking I might sneak into your room tonight."

The idea of making love to Beth in his bed thrilled him unreasonably. "What if we still have lingering guests?"

She gave him a tempting smile. "Then we'll be very, very quiet."

That put a vivid mental picture in his head. He could imagine making love to Beth, taking care not to make a single sound as they reached that moment of unparalleled pleasure together. He had lots more to learn about this lady. He slipped his hand beneath the hem of her blouse and fingered the tiny gold ring at her belly button. She shivered. He closed his hand around her waist and pressed another kiss to her sweet lips.

"Until tonight," he promised.

They'd been together every night during the past week, but it wasn't enough. Zach felt certain that a dozen lifetimes would never be long enough for him to get his fill of making love with Beth.

If only he didn't have to leave tomorrow.

"Pardon me, lovebirds."

Zach looked up, as did Beth, to find his mother approaching. He smiled. "Sorry, Mother. I try to restrain myself in public, but Beth just won't keep her hands off me."

Beth elbowed him in the gut. He grunted.

Colleen rolled her eyes. "I'll reserve comment." She turned to Beth. "You left your cell phone on the kitchen counter. When it rang I felt obliged to answer."

"Thank you." Surprised, Beth took the phone. She wasn't on call today. She glanced at the display to see who the caller was before she answered. The hospital. She frowned. She hoped the Ellroy girl hadn't been readmitted.

"Hey, Beth, it's Cindy."

The lab results.

Beth's internal thermometer plummeted. Ice slid through her veins. "Hey, Cindy."

"Well, I got around to your test. It's positive." There was a moment of silence. "Who's the lucky father?"

Beth moved away from Zach. "I appreciate you calling. I'll talk to you on Monday."

"Oh, I get it," Cindy said knowingly. "He's with you."

Beth glanced over her shoulder at Zach who was

still caught up in conversation with his mother. "Yeah, he is. Thanks for letting me know, Cindy."

"What're you going to do?"

The distress in her friend's voice echoed her own. "I don't know. I'll see you Monday."

Beth closed the phone and blinked back the tears that wanted to rise. What a mess she'd created. Every other time except that once she and Zach had used protection. But once was all it took. She knew that. And there was definitely no point in crying about it now.

It was done.

She was pregnant.

Now all she had to do was decide how she was going to tell Zach. If she told him at all.

She closed her eyes and held on to the warmth that just the memory of making love with him kindled inside her. She loved him so very much. If there'd ever been any doubt, the third time he'd made love to her had erased that possibility. She'd come home from work too tired to talk and too drained emotionally to feel. An elderly patient of hers had died despite her best efforts to save the woman. Advanced age and severe heart disease had rendered her efforts futile.

Zach had insisted on taking care of her. He'd gone home for a few minutes, then he'd returned for her. His mother was out for the evening so he'd turned her master bath into a getaway for Beth. Scented candles had encircled the huge garden tub. The slight breeze from the open window had made their flames dance. He'd slowly undressed her, taking time to massage her tense muscles. Then he'd assisted her into the hot depths of the whirling water. There he'd served her wine, cheese and grapes. He'd left her to soak and enjoy. When he'd returned to help her dress and walk her home, she hadn't wanted to go. Taking her cue, he'd made love to her right there on the elegant marble floor.

Beth threaded her fingers through her hair and sighed wearily. What the hell was she going to do? Now she was keeping two secrets from Zach. The first was life-altering enough. But this...

Beth closed her eyes as Zach came up behind her and slid his arms around her waist.

"Everything okay?"

She nodded, not trusting her voice.

"I was worried that maybe Laurie Ellroy was sick again." He rested his chin on her shoulder. "You haven't mentioned her in the past couple of days."

"I spoke with her mother on Wednesday. She's doing as well as can be expected."

"Good." His palm flatted on her abdomen and he pressed her against him.

Beth squeezed her eyes shut to ward off the tears brimming all over again with him touching her that way.

"How about we take a walk? It's over an hour until the parade."

"Okay." She turned around and offered him her best smile. "You can tell me what's in that huge box for your mother."

He grinned and took her hand. "You'll just have to wait and see like everyone else."

COLLEEN CHECKED her reflection in the mirror once more. She'd purchased a lovely pale lavender suit for the occasion. The cut of the suit was both flattering to her figure and youthful looking. The color highlighted rather than washed out her coloring. She was pleased with what she saw.

"Pretty good for an old lady," she mused aloud. If only Zacharius was still here.

She sat down at her dressing table and struggled again with the horrible weight sagging her shoulders. She simply could not tell her son the truth. No matter what Helen said, no matter what anyone said. She'd written the letter to be opened at her death. That would tell Zach everything he needed to know. Then she wouldn't be around to see his confusion or to feel the withdrawal of the love he gave so freely. She couldn't bear the thought of him looking at her in a different light. He was her son. She was his mother. She didn't want it to be any other way. Besides, she was seventy-five years old. How many more years on this earth could she have?

She'd be damned if she'd spend even one moment feeling as if her son no longer loved her or viewed her as his mother.

Not for Helen.

Not for anyone.

Colleen stood and walked determinedly from her bedroom. This was her day. She intended to enjoy it.

At the bottom of the stairs Betty waited for her. She'd been on vacation this past week. Betty served as housekeeper and assistant of sorts to Helen. The woman was much younger than either Colleen or Helen, but she was dependable and an excellent housekeeper.

"Mrs. Ashton, I was just about to come up and get you. You have a visitor in the parlor."

Colleen smiled. A visitor? Had Harold arrived early to give her his present in private?

"Thank you, Betty."

She nodded and scurried back to the kitchen where Helen was overseeing the caterer's work.

Signing contentedly, Colleen made her way to the parlor. She paused before entering and patted her hair. Harold was no Zacharius, but she did so enjoy his company.

She smiled widely and entered the room. "Hello, Har—" She halted abruptly, the rest of her words withering in her throat. Her heart jumped into an erratic rhythm, making her chest ache.

A woman stood waiting in the parlor. A woman Colleen would know anywhere, despite the passage of nearly four decades.

"What are you doing here?"

"I have to talk to you."

Jenny Ellroy looked haggard and pale and too old for her fifty-six years. Her hands trembled visibly so she clasped them in front of her. Colleen would have trembled herself had a kind of shock not set in the moment she laid eyes on her visitor.

"We have nothing to talk about," Colleen said shortly. "I'd like you to leave." She wondered briefly where Zach was. She didn't want him to see this woman. She didn't want him anywhere around to hear what was likely going to be said.

"I can't."

The pain and determination in those two words sent fear hurdling through Colleen. "You're trespassing. I didn't invite you here. Now you have to leave."

Jenny shook her head. "You have to help me."

"I don't have to do anything." Colleen stepped toward the woman in hopes of intimidating her somehow, but she just stood there, looking helpless and desperate.

"My daughter is dying."

A pang of sympathy ached through Colleen. "I'm sorry. If it's money you need, I'll be glad to help. You should have told me what you needed in the first place. I wouldn't turn my back on anyone in their time of need."

That was the truth if she'd ever told it. Colleen had spent her life helping others. The way she saw it, it was the least she could do after God had blessed her with such a perfect son.

Jenny shook her head. "I don't need your money, Mrs. Ashton." She blinked furiously, battling the tears Colleen could see shining in her eyes. "I need my son."

The room tilted a bit and Colleen clutched at the back of the sofa. Her heart pounded so fiercely she thought it might burst from her chest. "He's my son, not yours."

"My husband is dead," Jenny went on as if Colleen had said nothing.

"So is mine," she challenged. "But I still have *my* son."

"Due to my own health problems I'm useless to help my daughter."

Colleen held on to the back of the sofa, feeling more unsteady by the moment. "I don't know why you're telling me all this."

"My daughter, Laurie," she began, "has leukemia. Without a bone marrow transplant she's going to die."

Sweet Jesus, Colleen knew exactly what the woman wanted then. "I'm sorry, but this doesn't concern me or my son."

As if Colleen had said nothing, Jenny continued, "When his father came back alive from that POW camp I was so relieved that he was alive and that he still wanted me." She shook her head slowly. "I couldn't tell him I'd given his son away. How could I?" She sighed wearily. "Later we had a beautiful daughter. And now she's dying." She hesitated, her eyes settling on Colleen's. "He's her only hope. He'll surely be a match."

Fear and anger rocketed inside Colleen. "I will not spend my final days on this earth with my son calling another woman mother. Do you hear me? I won't do it."

"But you have to help me," Jenny pleaded. "He is my biological son."

"You gave up your rights to him a very long time ago. He has not been your son since the day you accepted my cashier's check and turned him over to me."

Color darkened the woman's pale cheeks. "So you're just going to let my daughter die?"

"I'm sorry for you and your daughter. But you can't be absolutely certain he'd be a match anyway. I won't risk everything for a mere chance. Now if you don't mind I'd like you to leave. This is my birthday and I don't want to be upset any further."

Jenny stepped toward her. Colleen tensed.

Their gazes locked and Jenny shook her head slowly from side to side. "How old are you today, Mrs. Ashton, seventy? Seventy-five?"

Colleen didn't answer. She wanted Jenny Ellroy to leave now and never come back.

"My daughter is twenty-two years old. She should have her whole life to look forward to, but she doesn't. She's going to die if she doesn't find a donor. Are you so selfish that you won't risk facing the consequences of our actions for the innocent life of a woman poised on the verge of her whole life?"

The mixture of emotions twisting inside Colleen held her silent. She couldn't speak.

Jenny Ellroy left without saying goodbye.

Colleen closed her eyes and fought the tidal wave bearing down on her. Dear God, what was she going to do? If she didn't tell Zach the truth...?

But how could she?

"What are you going to do?"

Colleen turned to face Helen. "Go away, Helen, I don't want to talk right now."

Helen looked almost as pale as the Ellroy woman had. "I heard all of it. You have to tell Zach the truth. You can't let that girl die. Do you hear me, Colleen? You can't let that girl die."

"You think I don't know that?" Colleen snarled.

"Then tell me what you're going to do," Helen pressed, her tone urgent, filled with fear for a girl they didn't even know.

Colleen met Helen's gaze. "I honestly don't know."

She'd sworn she wouldn't risk her son's love for anyone...not for anything.

"YOU THINK she looks okay?" Zach looked to Beth for confirmation of his concern. His mother looked rigid and on the verge of tears.

Beth didn't look at him. He frowned. "Beth, do you know something you're not telling me? Is my mother not feeling well and going on with this celebration anyway?"

"Maybe all the excitement has been more than she anticipated," Beth suggested. "But she assured me that she isn't having any worrisome symptoms. I asked how she was feeling earlier. I'd tell you if she'd even hinted at feeling any discomfort."

Zach wasn't convinced. His mother looked ready to burst into tears on her birthday when the whole town had turned out to honor her and Beth was behaving strangely as well.

Beth squeezed his arm. "You have to admit, this has been a rather long day." She offered a smile that fell short of her usual sincere beam.

"Yeah. I guess you're right."

After the parade the whole crowd had gathered around the gazebo for the official party. Lucky for Zach and Beth it hadn't rained and their decorating job still looked top-notch. Zach only wished he could say the same for his mother. Usually she loved attention. He just didn't get it. Something had to be wrong.

A drum roll sounded and Mayor Chadwick tapped the microphone to get everyone's attention.

"Now, ladies and gents, it's time for that special moment when we would generally sing 'Happy Birthday' to the birthday girl. But for this special occasion, Mr. Zach Ashton has offered to sing to his mother accompanied only by Viola on the piano."

Viola hit a high note on the piano they'd moved onto the lawn for the occasion.

Beth patted Zach's arm. "Don't worry, big guy, you'll do fine."

Zach grinned half-heartedly. "I've been practicing in the shower."

Beth smiled, the image of Zach naked in the shower and singing in that deep baritone was enough to chase even the worst of her worries away. "It'll make your mother's day," she murmured softly. At the moment Beth knew Mrs. Ashton needed reassurance from her son even if he didn't know that's what he was giving.

"I'm banking on it." He winked and pushed his way through the crowd until he stood before the gazebo. His mother sat in the place of honor, a glass of champagne in her hand.

Beth moved along the fringes until she was closer. She wanted to see and hear every moment of this. Zach looked so handsome in his navy suit. Her chest tightened at how the events about to unfold were likely going to affect him. And they were definitely going to unfold. There was no way Mrs. Ashton could keep this secret. She knew it and so did Beth now.

The news that Laurie Ellroy was his sister and that Zach most likely possessed the power to save her life had almost floored Beth. Her mother had told her about the conversation between Mrs. Ellroy and Colleen. Colleen had then insisted that Beth tell her everything she knew about Laurie. It was no wonder Colleen looked ready to fall apart any moment.

Beth could only imagine how it felt to be in Colleen's shoes. Beth felt badly enough knowing she'd played even a small part in keeping the truth from him. She could only pray that he would forgive her.

Beth thought of her other predicament and wondered what else could happen?

With the first line out of Zach's mouth complete silence overtook the crowd. Viola fingered the keys adding only a hint of melody to accompany his deep, rich voice. The tender yet strong way he sang the words combined with the sincere expression on his face tugged at Beth's heart. Mrs. Ashton looked captivated. Tears rolled down Beth's cheeks. Hard as she tried she just couldn't hold them back. All their lives were about to change for one reason or another and nothing would ever be the same.

Life as Zach knew it was about to end. All that he believed about himself and his family would come into question. She prayed that he would allow her to be there for him. She didn't even want to think about how the other news she had was going to affect him.

Beth shook off her haunting thoughts and focused all her attention on the man she loved and his heart-rending act of affection for his mother.

When he finished, everyone remained silent for one long moment, awed by the sweet sentiment. In that moment of calm, Zach bent down and kissed his mother's cheek. "Happy birthday, Mother. I love you."

A roaring ovation followed. Beth could hardly hear herself think for the cheers and thunderous clapping. Zach bowed to the crowd, then to his mother, blowing her yet another kiss.

Colleen stood, the look of pain on her face sent Beth running toward the gazebo. She could hear Zach asking his mother if she was all right, or maybe

Beth read his lips. The cheering and clapping faded into the background as she pushed through the crowd. Just as she reached the steps leading to the gazebo, Colleen collapsed in her son's arms.

Chapter Thirteen

"Just tell me what it means," Zach demanded.

Beth tried to be calm for him, but it was hard. She wanted to cry...she wanted to hold him, but he'd slipped into his attorney persona the moment the cardiologist came out and announced that Mrs. Ashton needed emergency surgery. The attending E.R. physician had called in the same cardiologist who had cared for Mrs. Ashton last time. Now the necessary preparations would be made and then Zach would be allowed to see his mother briefly before they took her to the operating room.

"It means," Beth began, struggling for composure, "that your mother opted not to have surgery after her first cardiac episode even though her doctor recommended it—"

"She what?" he roared. "Did you know about this?"

Beth shook her head. "No. If I had I would have called you."

Zach flung his arms out in exasperation. "Why does she have to be so damned hardheaded?"

"Anyway, now it's no longer an option. She has to have the surgery or..." Beth sighed.

Zach closed his eyes then pressed his fingertips there. "When are they going to let me see her?" He raked his fingers through his hair and started to pace again.

"I'm sure it won't be long."

Helen was almost as bad as Zach. She was pacing, wringing her hands and pacing.

Beth knew that at Mrs. Ashton's age the surgery was a little riskier, but her chances of recovery were very good. Beth knew how Zach felt. She trekked her mother's nervous pacing. If it was Helen in there…

In all the havoc that had followed Mrs. Ashton's collapse, Beth had forgotten, for just a little while, the terrible secret weighing so heavily on the three of them. The additional stress hadn't helped Colleen. Beth wished she had known about the suggested surgery before. Maybe she could have prevented this emergency procedure.

"Mr. Ashton." A stout nurse stepped from the trauma room. "You may see your mother for a few moments. But be very careful not to overexcite her."

Zach nodded his understanding. With a fleeting glance at Beth he rushed into the room where Mrs. Ashton was being medicated in preparation for surgery.

Beth turned to her mother then. Helen shook her head. "What are we going to do?" she asked wearily.

"I don't know." Beth put her arms around her and drew her close. "I just don't know."

HIS MOTHER looked so pale and fragile. Nothing like the woman he'd known his entire life. He wanted to somehow protect her from all this. Zach surveyed the array of beeping medical instruments and wires and tubes attached to his mother. He closed his eyes and said another quick prayer. He wasn't ready to lose her. Not yet.

"Zach."

His eyes opened at the weak whisper of his mother's voice. He took her hand in his and smiled. "Don't worry, everything's going to be fine. The doctor said—"

She shook her head. "Listen to me. I don't have much time."

"Don't say that," he protested gently. "The doctor—"

"I have to tell you," she interrupted again. Every word was a struggle.

The sedative was obviously already doing its work. "Okay," he relented. "I'm listening."

She licked her lips and tears brightened her eyes. Zach's heart squeezed. He didn't want her to cry. "Please don't cry," he pleaded.

"Do you know how much I love you?" she whispered.

He nodded, suddenly unable to speak.

"Your father and I loved you from the moment we laid eyes on you. You were everything we'd ever wanted."

"I know." He couldn't fathom why she was telling him this right now, but he would listen to whatever she had to say.

"But we were wrong." She took a shuddering breath. Zach tensed. "We made a mistake."

"Maybe you shouldn't talk anymore," he offered,

his worry increasing with every hampered breath she took.

She smiled faintly. "But we thought we were doing the right thing. We really did."

Maybe the sedative was making her brain fuzzy.

"But it was wrong. I know that now." She clutched his hand. "Promise me that you'll love me anyway."

"Of course I'll love you," he insisted, then laughed. "Hey, would I have made a fool of myself in front of the whole town like that if I didn't love you?"

She shook her head. "I mean after you know the truth. Promise me you'll love me after you know the truth."

His brow furrowed. "Truth? What truth? I don't understand."

"It was the right thing," she murmured. "I know in my heart that it was...but we should have told you. Helen warned me."

"Mr. Ashton."

Zach looked over his shoulder to find the nurse who'd allowed him into the room waiting at the door. "Can you give me another minute?" he pleaded.

"I'm sorry, Mr. Ashton, but the doctor's waiting. We really need to get Mrs. Ashton to surgery now."

Zach kissed his mother's forehead and squeezed her hand gently. "I love you. Please be strong for me."

She drew him back when he would have moved away. "Helen will tell you," she murmured, her voice almost too thick to understand now. "She knows. Make her tell you the rest."

Zach stood back as his mother was loaded onto a

gurney and wheeled out of the room. He wiped his eyes with the back of his hand and followed her into the corridor. He could only stand there after that and watch them take her away. There was nothing else he could do.

"She's going to be all right." Beth came up beside him and put her arms around him.

He draped his arm around her shoulder and thanked God that he had her. He wasn't sure he could do this alone.

"Why don't we go get some coffee," she suggested. "We're in for a long wait."

"Just a minute." His mother's strange comments surfaced through his worry. Zach turned to Helen. "Mother tried to tell me something, but the sedative had made her too drowsy. She kept telling me that she'd made a mistake." He shook his head. "None of it made sense. She said you would tell me." He looked down at Beth, confusion ruling his whole universe.

Beth froze. This was the moment she'd dreaded since her mother told her the truth. There was no way to take back the fact that she'd kept this horrible truth from Zach.

"We'll need to sit down," Helen suggested. "You don't want to hear this standing up."

The three of them made their way to a private waiting room on the floor. It was the one provided for families who needed privacy to make the kind of decisions no one wanted to think about much less face.

The upholstered chairs sat in a kind of circle, allowing all seated to make eye contact without having to turn to look at the person seated next to them.

Beth suddenly wished she didn't have to see what would be in Zach's eyes when he heard what Helen had to say.

But she had no choice. He knew they were keeping something from him. There would be no bowing out gracefully.

"There's no easy way to say this, Zach," Helen began. "But the short of it is that your mother couldn't have children. So she and I made a deal with a young woman who was unmarried and pregnant. That's how you came to be an Ashton. Colleen and Zacharius brought you home from the hospital when you were four days old and you've been theirs ever since."

Zach shook his head. "That's impossible." The whole concept was ludicrous. She couldn't mean...

Helen sighed. "I'm afraid it's the truth. That's what Colleen and I have been at war about. I thought she should tell you and she didn't."

This was insane. Zach stood. He shook his head again. "You're telling me that I'm adopted."

"Well, not exactly. There was no adoption. Your birth mother signed in at the hospital as Colleen Ashton, so as far as the rest of the world knows you are an Ashton."

Zach laughed, the sound choked and dry. "So I was purchased from an unwed mother?" He felt numb or cold...or maybe both.

Helen nodded resignedly. "That's about the size of it." She fixed him with a firm gaze. "But Colleen and Zacharius loved you like their own and gave you anything you ever needed or wanted, and don't you ever forget it."

He shook his head again in an effort to clear it. "You're serious?"

Helen nodded a second time.

Zach scrubbed a hand over his face and turned to Beth who'd remained conspicuously silent thus far. "Did you know about this?"

"Yes."

He swore…one of those crude four-letter words he rarely used. The woman he'd been making love with all week knew his whole life was a sham and she hadn't bothered to tell him.

"How did you know when I didn't?" he demanded.

Beth jerked at his sharp tone. "I only found out a few days ago," she explained.

A dozen emotions twisted inside him, combining then erupting into one fierce bolt of fury that instantly replaced the numbness. "And it never once occurred to you while we were making love to tell me this little seemingly insignificant fact."

"Zach, I'm sorry. I didn't want to keep it from you, but—"

"It's not her fault," Helen cut in. "We were both obeying your mother's wishes. If you can fault us for that, then have at it."

"And this birth mother," he spat savagely. "What became of her?"

Helen looked at Beth, who looked downright stricken.

"I want to know," he commanded. "Who the hell is the woman who gave birth to me?"

Beth stood then, meeting his gaze with a kind of resignation that tore at his heart. Dammit, why had everyone been keeping secrets from him? This whole thing was nuts.

"Your biological mother is Jenny Ellroy. Her daughter, Laurie, is your sister. I didn't know until today."

Zach blinked, stunned. The dying girl was his sister? The woman who'd acted so strangely from the moment he told her his name was his birth mother? This couldn't be happening. He knew who he was. There had to be a mistake.

"And," Beth went on, a tremble in her voice, "you're probably one of the few people on earth who might be able to save her life."

Zach shook his head, fury, hurt, disappointment, disbelief all exploding inside him like a Fourth of July fireworks display. He was thirty-eight years old. He knew who he was…where he'd come from. His father and his mother had always been there for him. There'd never been any question.

"I'm so sorry you had to hear it this way," Beth said, dragging his attention back to the tiny waiting room.

The walls seemed to close in around him. He felt sick to his stomach. He shook his head in denial of it all. "I…" He backed toward the door. "I don't want to know this."

THE CAFETERIA was practically deserted when Beth finally made her way there. She wasn't hungry, but a cup of hot chocolate was definitely in order. Helen had gone back to the house to see that Betty and Mayor Chadwick took care of everything. She'd insisted that Colleen would not want to go home to disorder. Beth knew her mother simply needed to be doing something. Colleen would be out of surgery any time now. And then Beth would have to face Zach again. As she settled at one of the empty tables, she prayed the hot, creamy liquid in her cup would somehow shore up her courage for their next encounter.

She hadn't seen him since he walked out of that private waiting room. She knew he wasn't far away. But he obviously didn't want to see or talk to her. She swallowed at the lump rising in her throat. The thought of the child they'd conceived made her want to cry all over again. But she'd already done that. She had to hold herself together at this point. She stared into her cup as if it held some sort of answer.

For hours now she'd berated herself for not telling Zach the truth as soon as her mother told her. But how could she? He would surely have confronted his mother and perhaps brought on the very episode she'd suffered today. Zach would never have been able to live with that kind of guilt. Beth had done the right thing…but what would she do now? He might never forgive her for not telling him the truth whether it was the right thing to do or not. Not to mention she had this other secret hanging in the balance. He was so confused right now. Everything he'd ever thought to be true would come into question if only in his own mind.

How could she throw him this new curve?

She couldn't.

Not right now anyway.

Beth massaged her temples with her fingertips. Her head was pounding. Her stomach felt as if it was tied in a thousand knots. What was she going to do now?

"Is this seat taken?"

Her breath caught as she looked up to find Zach. She shook her head. "No…it's not taken."

He looked so tired but like heaven on earth to her weary eyes.

"Where's Helen?" He sat down in the chair directly across from her.

At least he was talking to her. "She went back to the house to make sure everything was cleaned up and secure."

He nodded. "Good."

He stared at her cup for so long Beth was sure he'd fallen asleep with his eyes open. "Would you like some hot chocolate or coffee?" she suggested.

Seemingly startled, his gaze connected with hers. "No. I'm fine. She's in recovery now," he added almost as an afterthought. "The doctor said everything went exceptionally well. I can see her in a little while." He resumed his steady stare at the white foam cup on the table.

Relief flowed swiftly through Beth. "Thank God." She tried not to tag any significance to his calling Colleen "she" and "her" rather than "mother." He was just confused. Zach was strong, extremely intelligent and one of the most compassionate men she'd ever known. He wouldn't let this ruin his relationship with Colleen. Beth believed that with all her heart. Though she couldn't be sure where she stood with him.

"This will all work out, Zach," she felt compelled to say after an awkward moment of silence.

He lifted an emotionless gaze back to hers. "I know."

She suddenly wanted to tell him everything. That she loved him more than anything else in this world and that they'd made a baby. She moistened her lips and tried her level best not to let him see her tremble. She blinked back the tears that wanted to well in her eyes. Now was not the time.

"She'll die without a suitable donor?" he asked suddenly.

She. Not Laurie, not my sister. She. Beth could only imagine how much he was hurting inside. Those somber blue eyes gave nothing away. The light that was Zach Ashton was so very dim right now, it was like looking at a stranger.

"Yes," she told him. "Laurie will die." Beth knotted her hands together in her lap to keep from reaching out to him. He didn't want her right now...he might never again. "She could still die even if a suitable donor is found. But, slim as it is, it's the only chance she has."

His haunted gaze remained steady on hers. "What's the chances of my being a suitable donor?"

Beth tried not to get her hopes up. She wanted so badly for Laurie to have this chance at life, but at the same time she knew what this was costing Zach. "The chances are excellent. You share the same... biological mother and father. It'd be a fluke if you weren't compatible."

"How do we find out if I'm the right match?"

We? Hope soared in her chest. He wasn't leaving her out completely. "There's a simple test that will tell us."

He stood, then shoved his hands into the pockets of his trousers. "I should be able to see her by now." He turned to go.

Beth rose, tempted to run after him. "What about the test?"

He paused and turned back to her, then hesitated again. "Yeah." He nodded slowly. "Set it up."

The tears would not be restrained as she watched him walk away. His entire personal life was falling apart and still he'd decided to help this young woman. A woman he really didn't even know despite the fact that she was his sister.

Beth smiled. She hadn't expected anything less. This was just the kind of man Zach Ashton was. It was the Ashton in him. A sob escaped her. And he was definitely an Ashton.

HE'D GONE BY the lab and parted with the necessary sample. Beth had stopped by Colleen's room later to let him know the results. He was a match. She'd left immediately afterward, not asking questions or lingering to try and draw out conversation. As much as he cared for her, Zach had been glad. He needed to think.

Now, exhausted by his troubling thoughts, he sat at Colleen's bedside. She looked so pale and fragile still. He struggled with the tears stinging his eyes. He didn't want her to wake up and find him blubbering like a baby—even if he did feel like doing just that. The doctor had assured him that she was going to be fine. She was strong and in excellent health otherwise.

How could his whole life be built on one big deception?

He closed his eyes and sighed wearily. Did it really matter how his life started out? He opened his eyes and looked at the woman who'd cared for him and loved him every day of his life. No. Only one thing mattered.

He stood and leaned down to kiss her cheek. When he drew back her eyes drifted open. He smiled. "Welcome back." He gritted his teeth and with the heel of his hand rubbed fiercely at the one tear that managed to escape his brutal hold.

Her gray eyes grew misty. "You know?" she said simply.

He nodded. "Yes."

She reached for his hand, hers too cold and far too weak for his liking. "I'm sorry. I didn't mean for any of this to hurt you."

He shook his head, fighting a new wave of liquid emotion. "There's nothing to be sorry for. I'm a big boy I can take anything life throws my way." A tear slipped down her face. He gently wiped it away. "I don't want you to cry."

"I didn't set out to deceive you. I loved you so much I couldn't bear the thought of you thinking any less of me or seeing me as anything other than your real mother. I was wrong." She took a deep, halting breath. "I should have told you so that you could make up your own mind. I was selfish. I didn't consider that they might need you, too."

Zach kissed her hand, then her forehead. "Don't worry. I'll do the right thing." He smiled that cocky gesture he'd learned from his father. "I'm an Ashton. We always do the right thing. But there's something *you* have to understand and it comes from right here." He pressed her hand over his heart, then covered it with his own. "You are my mother. No one else will ever hold that place in my heart."

ON THE ELEVATOR ride down to the lobby, Zach made a decision. He knew what he had to do to set his life to rights and he intended to do it today. Now if he could just find Beth. Helen had arrived to sit with his mother and she'd told him that Beth was helping out in the E.R. for a couple of hours. Apparently the duty physician had fallen ill and since Beth was in the hospital already she'd offered to hang around a few hours and finish his shift.

Zach smiled. That was just like Beth. Always putting everyone else ahead of herself. He glanced at his watch—6:30 a.m. If the guy's shift ended at seven, then Beth would be free in a few minutes.

The elevator doors glided open and he stepped out into the spacious atrium style lobby. The corridor on the other side of the room would lead to the E.R. the nurse who'd come to take his mother's vitals had told him.

"Mr. Ashton."

Zach stopped halfway to his destination and turned back to see who'd called his name.

Jenny Ellroy stood a few feet away. Zach tensed. He wasn't sure he was ready for this meeting yet. Her thin, weary features struck him anew. Something stirred inside him, in a place too far away to touch or understand. "Mrs. Ellroy," he returned.

"I wanted to see how...your...mother was doing."

Zach knew what she was thinking. He could see it in her eyes. She was trying to decide if he knew the truth yet or not. "My mother is doing well. The doctor says she's going to be fine."

Mrs. Ellroy sighed with obvious relief. "I'm glad." She studied Zach's face. "And you? How are you holding up?"

"I'm hanging in there," he told her frankly.

She nodded. "Well, I'll be going then. I just wanted to see that Mrs. Ashton was all right."

He wondered if she had reason to feel as guilty as she looked. Had something gone down between her and his mother recently? He'd have to ask Beth.

He almost let Mrs. Ellroy walk away. But he couldn't. As much as he resented her somehow…in a way that didn't even make sense to him right now, he couldn't allow her and her daughter to believe that there was still no hope.

"I took the test."

She turned back to him, her eyes growing wide with hope. "The test?" she asked, feigning innocence still to no doubt spare his feelings in the event he didn't know.

"I'm a perfect match. I told Beth to have your daughter's doctor set up the transplant."

She didn't respond for a time. He could see the difficulty she was having maintaining her composure. She trembled visibly and tears had gathered in her eyes.

"Thank you," she finally managed.

He acknowledged her gratitude with a nod.

She started to turn away again and Zach stopped her once more. "You did the right thing, you know."

Tears glistened on her cheeks as a kind of unspoken understanding passed between them.

"Now," Zach continued, a new rush of emotion crowding his chest, "I have the opportunity to repay you for what you did for me."

"I won't ever forget it," she said softly then turned away once more.

This time he let her go. He watched until she'd

exited the building. There were other things that needed to be said, but not right now.

Right now, he had to do the right thing by Beth.

The things he had to say to her had been a long time in coming. He could only hope that she would consider it worth the wait.

Chapter Fourteen

"Beth, can you see one last patient before you go?"

Beth dredged up a smile. "Sure."

"He's in five."

Dead on her feet, Beth trudged toward exam room five. Phillips owed her big time for this. But he would have done the same for her, she supposed, had she been on duty and been hit by an unexpected bug. Patients didn't respond well to sweating and vomiting doctors.

Besides, she had to admit that it had been quiet other than the car accident victim and even his injuries had been relatively minor. Beth definitely couldn't complain. As E.R. duty went, this had been a piece of cake. And it kept her mind off Zach. She'd already called the nurse's station and checked on Mrs. Ashton. She was stable and resting. They'd probably send her home in a couple of days if all continued as expected.

Beth frowned when she found no chart in the box on the door of exam room five. Maybe the nurse had simply forgotten and left it in the room with the patient. She opened the door and entered the room.

"Good morning, I'm Dr. Daniels."

"I think it's time you stopped using your ex's name."

Zach.

What was he doing here?

Worry etched across her forehead. "Are you all right?" she demanded. Maybe the stress had gotten to him and he'd started having chest pains of his own. Fear streaked through her.

He shook his handsome head. "Nope. I'm not sure I'll ever be all right again."

Beth moved closer to him, studying his face, his posture, for signs of discomfort. "Are you in pain?"

Leaning against the exam table with his arms folded over his chest, he looked relaxed enough. "Not really."

"Then what's wrong?" She ordered her heart to slow its pounding. It felt ready to catapult out of her chest.

"I just wanted to see you. The nurse said this would be the best way."

Beth passed a hand over her face and sighed her relief. "Jesus, Zach, you scared the hell out of me."

He pulled her into his arms. "Sorry." When she was settled intimately against him he demanded, "Now, do you agree about the name thing?"

Oh, yes. Her ex's name. "I'm working on that."

He nodded. "Good. It's past time."

Why did he care what name she used? She tried not to get her hopes up here. Though he appeared his usual caring self, there was still other life-altering news with which he would have to contend.

"I assume this means you're not angry with me anymore?" She searched those amazing blue eyes and that equally amazing face. She held her breath as she waited for his answer.

"I've done a lot of thinking. And I know this isn't your fault. I was wrong to take any part of it out on you."

That was too easy. Worry crept back into her heart. "So you're okay with all this?"

He shrugged. "I don't know if I'm okay with it, but I understand that there's nothing I can do about it." He looked thoughtful for a moment. "I guess I'm in a kind of shock. But still, I do know who I am. As crazy as it sounds, this doesn't change that...not in my opinion anyway."

Beth relaxed and snaked her arms around his lean waist. "I'm glad you're dealing with it this way."

"I'm sure there will be times when I won't see things so clearly, but I was hoping you'd be around to help me through those times."

She swallowed tightly. Would he want her around when she told him her news? "I'll be around."

He smoothed a handful of hair over her shoulder, then allowed that hand to glide down her spine, sending goose bumps over her skin. "There's something I need to tell you, Beth, and I'm not sure how to begin."

Her heart bumped back into a rapid staccato. "The beginning is usually the best place," she offered. Please don't let this be about letting her down easy, she prayed.

He angled his head and studied her face and eyes for a time before he spoke. Just when she thought she wouldn't be able to bear his gaze on her a moment longer, he spoke.

"I think I've always loved you, but I fell in love

with you the day you modeled the dress your mother had made you for your first prom.''

Beth didn't know what to say. Emotion welled inside her to the point of making any kind of breath an impossibility.

''I'd come home for the weekend from school,'' he continued. ''You were all excited about being invited to the prom by a junior.'' He laughed. ''God, I was so damned jealous I couldn't see straight. And when I saw you in that dress I knew. I was too old for you, of course, and I felt like a slimeball for having those feelings. But no matter how hard I tried I just couldn't make them go away.''

Beth swiped away a tear that slipped past her hold. ''I didn't know.''

He pressed his forehead to hers. ''I know. I thought waiting was the right thing to do.'' He sighed. ''So I waited for you to grow up.''

''But when I kissed you I was seventeen and you—''

''Made a mistake,'' he interjected. ''I should have told you then how I felt and why we had to wait. But I thought we had all the time in the world. And I didn't want to do the wrong thing.'' He frowned. ''You were so young.''

Beth stared at him in disbelief. ''Oh, my God. Are you telling me that—''

''You broke my heart when you married that jerk Daniels,'' he said pointedly.

Her hand went to her mouth. ''I'm sorry,'' she offered. ''I was only trying to forget about you.''

His frown deepened. ''Forget about me?''

She nodded. ''I've been in love with you since I was twelve years old, Zach. Surely you noticed.''

"Well." He shrugged. "I knew you liked me, but I was afraid you'd outgrown it."

"And what about now?" She pinned him with a firm look.

"I know you care about me, but you didn't really anticipate anything coming of it. Am I right?"

"Zach Ashton, you are so blind," she accused. "I got my belly button pierced for you!"

He grinned. "You did that for me?"

She frowned petulantly. "I wanted to prove to you that I wasn't such a *good* girl. I wanted you to know that I was a woman who had needs. I can't believe this," she protested. "How could you not know how much I love you?"

He looked amused by her confession, but still confused by his own feelings. "I guess I've been afraid to trust my instincts where you're concerned."

"Afraid? I can't believe you're admitting that."

He pulled her closer, leaving nothing to chance when it came to his feelings. He wanted her to know how he felt. There was no way to miss it. He was fully, undeniably aroused.

"I don't want there to be any more deceptions between me and the people I love."

Beth faltered. She had to tell him.

"The truth is," he confessed, "I wasn't going to tell you how I felt. I'd planned to go back to Chicago and put it all, including you, behind me. You belong here, I could see that. You love your work. I didn't want to ask you to choose."

She stilled. "What changed your mind?"

"Life is too short and I love you too much. I'm not spending the rest of my life without you unless it's your choice. It won't be mine."

Beth wanted to shout her happiness to the world. She wanted to throw her arms around his neck and kiss him senseless. But she couldn't…not until she'd told him.

"I have been considering that job offer," she ventured. "I'd planned to fly to Chicago next week and do the interview."

"You'd do that for me?" He looked so genuinely worried, and yet so hopeful.

"I'd do it for us. I love you, Zach. There is no other choice. Did you think I couldn't deal with change? I'm an adult, I can adapt."

"But your mother told my mother that you hated city life and that you never wanted to go back to it."

"I hated my life in Indianapolis because my marriage was falling apart. It had nothing to do with the city. I didn't want to go back to my old life, Zach, not the city itself."

"So staying here isn't a priority?"

How many ways did he want her to say it? "I love it here, yes, that's true. There are lots of things I prefer about small-town living over city life. But, I don't hate the city. I'll get used to it. The main thing is, that's where you are."

He kissed her. It went on forever. She could feel his yearning…his need. He'd been through so much. Now he wanted her reassurance. And she couldn't give it to him completely just yet.

When he drew back they were both breathless. "I love you. I don't want to leave without you."

"There's just one other thing," she said solemnly. "You might feel differently when I tell you."

He watched her intently, but his expression didn't grow guarded. He trusted her. Her heart skipped a beat with the emotion crowding her chest. She prayed this would be good news in his opinion. The fact that he wanted her in his life was a far cry from wanting children. He might not want children at all...or, at least, not anytime soon.

"Tell me," he urged. "Whatever it is, we'll find a way to work it out."

The sweetness of his words touched her. "We're pregnant."

"What?"

Uncertainty trickled through her. "That first time...well, I conceived."

"You're going to have a baby?" He gave his head a little shake. "How can you know this already?"

"After we'd...well, you know...done it, I realized that I was probably ovulating—"

He shook his head again. "You don't take the pill or something?"

She moistened her lips. "No. I hadn't been with anyone in over a year—"

"A year?" He looked positively stunned.

"I told you my marriage was falling apart and..." She shrugged. "Until you..."

"Go on," he encouraged, though he looked a tad uncertain.

She mustered her courage and went on. "Anyway, knowing what I knew about my cycle and not wanting any surprises later I had a blood test done. The hormone HCG shows up within days of conception."

"You're sure?"

She nodded. "I'm sorry, Zach. I didn't—"

A totally idiotic look claimed his face. "I'm going to be a daddy." He kissed her. "We have to tell somebody. Our mothers.'' He grinned from ear to ear. ''We have to tell them.''

Beth was the one who needed reassurances now. ''Wait. What are you saying here?''

He cupped her face in his hands. ''I'm saying that I want to marry you.'' He kissed her forehead. ''I'm saying that I want you to come back to Chicago with me and help me find the perfect house where we can raise our baby.''

''You're sure about all this?'' She held on to her heart a second longer.

''Absolutely positive.''

''Then, yes. Let's do it.'' She gave herself completely to him then, heart and soul. She pressed her lips to his in proof of her declaration.

''We should find some place where we won't be interrupted,'' he murmured between kisses. ''I want to consummate this deal right away.''

''I know just the place.''

Two minutes later, Beth had locked the door to the rarely used first floor doctor's lounge and Zach was using his mouth and hands to show her just what she could expect out of their future together.

ON WEDNESDAY Zach brought his mother home. She was happy to be free of what she called hell in a ten by twelve cell, and even happier to learn that he and Beth were getting married. By that same afternoon Colleen and Helen were already making wedding plans and arguing over who would get to keep the baby first.

Zach left them with their bickering and went to the cottage in search of Beth. She was fast asleep on the couch. The urge to kiss her was almost overwhelming, but he restrained himself. She'd worked late at the hospital last night and he knew she needed her rest.

He went to the kitchen and poured himself a glass of orange juice. He might as well give Victoria an update. She'd told him not to call until after his mother was home from the hospital. As much as the head of the Colby Agency missed him she didn't want him hurrying back to Chicago.

Victoria would really be surprised when he told her he wasn't returning alone. His love-'em-and-leave-'em reputation was history.

When Mildred told him that Ethan, one of their top investigators, was in the office with Victoria, Zach offered to call back later. Mildred informed him in her matter of fact way that Victoria had left explicit instructions that Zach was to be patched through no matter who was in her office. That brought a grin to Zach's face. No one, not even Mildred, and she'd been with the agency since its inception, went against Victoria's wishes.

"Zach, I hope this call means that your mother is doing well?" his boss said by way of a greeting.

"That she is. I brought her home today. She's already planning her next big celebration."

"I'm glad to hear it. When are you anticipating returning to the city?"

"I've booked an early flight for Friday morning."

"Excellent. We have a new case that requires your expertise."

Zach grinned as that old adrenaline began to flow. "Give me a few details."

"I'll put you on speaker and Ethan can fill you in."

"Hey, Zach-man, hope you've had enough of the good life because I've got a hot one here."

Ethan's laid-back, easygoing attitude and casual appearance were most effective in earning people's trust. Little did they know that the man was a former Special Forces member whose marksmanship skills were still renowned in the units he'd served. His hostage retrieval skills were the first to draw Victoria's attention. But it was the combination of good old boy presentation and unparalleled cunning that had cinched his position at the agency.

Leaning one hip against the counter, Zach listened, commenting occasionally, for the next few minutes as Ethan laid out his latest case.

"Sounds like you've got it nailed down," Zach offered. "That's the route I would take."

"Thanks. That's what I wanted to hear," Ethan said.

"We're looking forward to having you back in the office," Victoria added, then paused. "You mentioned that your mother was already planning her next celebration. Christmas?"

Zach grinned. He'd waited for this moment. "No, no. Christmas is still almost three months away."

"Don't keep us in suspense," Victoria prodded.

"She's helping plan my wedding, which is taking place next month."

"Your wedding?"

"Whoa! Zach-man. I can't believe it! Wait until I tell Ian and the guys."

"I expect a top-notch bachelor party," he informed Ethan.

"Consider it done, buddy."

"Oh, I see now," Victoria said knowingly. "So

you went back home and fell in love with the girl next door all over again, did you?''

Happiness swelled in Zach's chest. "Yeah. I did." She's a doctor, Zach didn't add. And she had just the prescription he needed.

The rest of the conversation was lost on Zach, because that good girl who'd lived next door to him for the first half of his life came into the room and kissed him soundly on the lips. He eventually managed a goodbye and hung up the phone.

Beth nipped his chin, then laved it with the tip of her tongue. "I thought we could make up for lost time since I was on duty last night."

"I hope you know I'll expect this treatment every time you work late," he murmured against her soft cheek.

"You can count on it," she whispered back. "I don't want to waste a single moment."

"They'll all be special," he promised as he kissed her nose, then her sweet lips. "Every moment of every day for the rest of our lives."

Epilogue

Early morning sunlight poured in through the rich stained glass windows. The priest's words echoed through the lofty cathedral in a way that only added to the spiritual ambiance. Beth blinked rapidly to hold back her tears of joy. Her heart was overflowing.

"I christen thee Charles Zacharius Ashton the third," the priest said as he dabbed the holy water on the baby's forehead. Little Zach wailed in protest.

Beth smiled down at her beautiful baby boy and then up at his handsome father. She loved them both so very much. She thanked God every day for their precious life together. This moment only exemplified all that she had to be grateful for.

Zach's gaze met hers and she saw in those blue eyes the same emotions she felt. He was just as happy as she was. She couldn't ask for anything more.

The priest presented Zach with his son and Beth's heart leapt. Zach placed a tender kiss on his son's forehead then offered him to Beth. Tears blurring her vision, Beth took her child in her arms and kissed him the same way his father had.

The family and friends gathered in the cathedral stood and moved forward to congratulate them. Victoria Colby and several of Zach's co-workers were there, including Alex Preston Hayden and her good-looking husband. Ethan Delaney, Ian Michaels and his lovely wife were there as well. Jenny Ellroy, Laurie and her new husband were present also. The bone marrow transplant had been a success and Laurie was doing amazingly well. Another prayer answered.

Where were their mothers? Beth frowned as she scanned the faces gathering around them for the two most important ones.

"Get out of my way, you old battle-ax!"

Beth's gaze collided with Zach's at the sound of her mother's heated words.

"I told you I was going to hold him first after the christening," Colleen snapped. "Now get out of my way or I'll run you over."

Colleen burst through the crowd, paused briefly to compose herself, then pasted a smile in place. Helen came up right behind her, annoyance marring her brow.

Zach leaned toward Beth and whispered, "Maybe we should have another one soon so they'll both have something to do."

Beth chewed her lower lip. "Well," she began, "I think that can be arranged a couple of months down the road."

His gaze sought hers, and the love she saw there filled her heart to overflowing. "That's a date." He leaned down and kissed her cheek. "Thank you," he murmured.

She arched a skeptical brow. "For penciling you in on my calendar?"

He shook his head. "For making me the happiest man alive."

* * * * *

You can find more Colby Agency *stories wherever Harlequin Intrigue books are sold.*

Continuing in September from

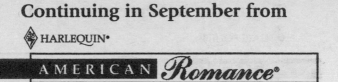

the heartwarming series by
Sharon Swan

**Come back to Harmony, Arizona,
a little town with lots of surprises!**

Abby Prentiss is about to walk down the aisle with the
perfect man...until her ex-husband shows up on the
doorstep of her bed-and-breakfast. But Ryan Larabee
doesn't know he was once married to Abby—because Ryan
has amnesia! What's a bride-to-be to do? Find out in...

HUSBANDS, HUSBANDS...EVERYWHERE!

*Available September 2002
wherever Harlequin books are sold.*

Visit us at www.eHarlequin.com   HARHHE

Beginning in September from

HARLEQUIN®

AMERICAN *Romance*®

Serving their country,
as they follow their hearts...

GROOMS IN UNIFORM

a new series of romantic adventure by
Mollie Molay

Enjoy all three titles in this new series:

A duchess crosses swords with the naval officer
assigned to protect her in

THE DUCHESS & HER BODYGUARD
On sale September 2002

A special-agent-in-charge surrenders his heart
to a feisty free spirit in

SECRET SERVICE DAD
On sale November 2002

Look for the third title in this delightful series in January 2003.

HARLEQUIN®
Makes any time special®

Visit us at www.eHarlequin.com

HARGIU

Coming in August...

UNBREAKABLE BONDS

by

Judy Christenberry

Identical twin brothers separated at birth. One had every opportunity imaginable. One had nothing, except the ties of blood. Now fate brings them back together as part of the Randall family, where they are thrown into a maelstrom of divided loyalties, unexpected revelations and the knowledge that some bonds are simply unbreakable.

Dive into a new chapter of the bestselling series *Brides for Brothers* with this unforgettable story.

Available August 2002 wherever paperbacks are sold.

HARLEQUIN®
Makes any time special ®

Visit us at www.eHarlequin.com

PHUB-R

Three masters of the romantic suspense
genre come together in this special
Collector's Edition!

Unveiled

NEW YORK TIMES BESTSELLING AUTHORS

TESS GERRITSEN
STELLA CAMERON

And Harlequin Intrigue® author

AMANDA STEVENS

Nail-biting mystery…heart-pounding sensuality…and
the temptation of the unknown come together in one
magnificent trade-size volume. These three talented
authors bring stories that will give you thrills *and*
chills like never before!

Coming to your favorite retail outlet in August 2002.

HARLEQUIN®
Makes any time special ®

Visit us at www.eHarlequin.com

PHU

If you enjoyed what you just read,
then we've got an offer you can't resist!

Take 2 bestselling
love stories FREE!
Plus get a FREE surprise gift!

Clip this page and mail it to Harlequin Reader Service®

IN U.S.A.	**IN CANADA**
3010 Walden Ave.	P.O. Box 609
P.O. Box 1867	Fort Erie, Ontario
Buffalo, N.Y. 14240-1867	L2A 5X3

YES! Please send me 2 free Harlequin American Romance® novels and my free surprise gift. After receiving them, if I don't wish to receive anymore, I can return the shipping statement marked cancel. If I don't cancel, I will receive 4 brand-new novels every month, before they're available in stores! In the U.S.A., bill me at the bargain price of $3.99 plus 25¢ shipping & handling per book and applicable sales tax, if any*. In Canada, bill me at the bargain price of $4.74 plus 25¢ shipping & handling per book and applicable taxes**. That's the complete price and a savings of at least 10% off the cover prices—what a great deal! I understand that accepting the 2 free books and gift places me under no obligation ever to buy any books. I can always return a shipment and cancel at any time. Even if I never buy another book from Harlequin, the 2 free books and gift are mine to keep forever.

154 HDN DNT7
354 HDN DNT9

Name	(PLEASE PRINT)	
Address		Apt.#
City	State/Prov.	Zip/Postal Code

* Terms and prices subject to change without notice. Sales tax applicable in N.Y.
** Canadian residents will be charged applicable provincial taxes and GST.
  All orders subject to approval. Offer limited to one per household and not valid to
  current Harlequin American Romance® subscribers.
  ® are registered trademarks of Harlequin Enterprises Limited.

AMER02   ©2001 Harlequin Enterprises Limited

eHARLEQUIN.com

community | membership

buy books | authors | online reads | magazine | learn to write

buy books

♥ We have your favorite books from Harlequin, Silhouette, MIRA and Steeple Hill, plus bestselling authors in Other Romances. Discover savings, find new releases and fall in love with past classics all over again!

online reads

♥ Read daily and weekly chapters from Internet-exclusive serials, and decide what should happen next in great interactive stories!

magazine

♥ Learn how to spice up your love life, play fun games and quizzes, read about celebrities, travel, beauty and so much more.

authors

♥ Select from over 300 Harlequin author profiles and read interviews with your favorite bestselling authors!

community

♥ Share your passion for love, life and romance novels in our online message boards!

learn to write

♥ All the tips and tools you need to craft the perfect novel, including our special romance novel critique service.

membership

♥ FREE! Be the first to hear about all your favorite themes, authors and series and be part of exciting contests, exclusive promotions, special deals and online events.

HARLEQUIN®

Makes any time special®—online...

Visit us at
www.eHarlequin.com

HINT7CH

HARLEQUIN®

AMERICAN *Romance*®

How do you marry a Hardison?

**First you tempt him. Then you tame him…
all the way to the altar.**

How to Marry **A HARDISON**

by

Kara Lennox

The handsome Hardison brothers are about to meet their matches when three Texas ladies decide to stop at nothing to lasso one of these most eligible bachelors.

Watch for:

VIXEN IN DISGUISE
August 2002

PLAIN JANE'S PLAN
October 2002

SASSY CINDERELLA
December 2002

Don't miss Kara Lennox's HOW TO MARRY A HARDISON series, available wherever Harlequin books are sold.

HARLEQUIN®
Makes any time special®

Visit us at www.eHarlequin.com

HARHTMAH

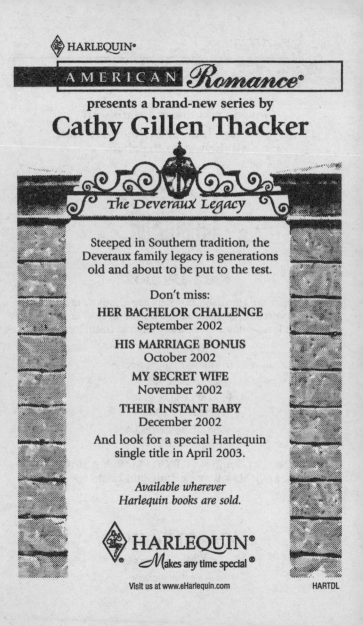

HARLEQUIN®

AMERICAN *Romance*®

presents a brand-new series by
Cathy Gillen Thacker

The Deveraux Legacy

Steeped in Southern tradition, the
Deveraux family legacy is generations
old and about to be put to the test.

Don't miss:

HER BACHELOR CHALLENGE
September 2002

HIS MARRIAGE BONUS
October 2002

MY SECRET WIFE
November 2002

THEIR INSTANT BABY
December 2002

And look for a special Harlequin
single title in April 2003.

*Available wherever
Harlequin books are sold.*

HARLEQUIN®
Makes any time special®

Visit us at www.eHarlequin.com

HARTDL